LUMPINI PARK

Chasing Chinatown Trilogy
Book Two

(Abby Kane FBI Thriller)

Ty Hutchinson

D1527302

Published by Ty Hutchinson
Copyright © 2014 by Ty Hutchinson
Cover Design: Damonza

For Appon

LUMPINI PARK

Chasing Chinatown Trilogy
Book Two

(Abby Kane FBI Thriller)

Chapter 1

The heat index that day was ninety-four degrees Fahrenheit. A fluke? Hardly. Every now and then, San Francisco becomes a hot, sticky mess—something Special Agent Scott Reilly would discover in less than forty minutes.

The assault team consisted of twelve men from the FBI Special Weapons and Tactical Team packed into two modified civilian vans. Reilly and four other agents followed in a black SUV.

Waverly Place was their destination, a small, alley-like street about fifty yards long, lined mostly with temples and a few shops. Mixed amongst the buildings were a couple of Chinese Benevolent Organizations, or tongs. The Hop Sing Tong was the target.

The street was bookended by the vans, and two tactical teams approached the building on foot. The area was unusually quiet for that time of day. A blessing? More like a sign. A hushed murmur of Chinese was the only sound heard as the two teams approached the small crowd of residents that had gathered outside the tong.

Team One was ordered to clear the crowd of looky-loos while Team Two, Reilly's team, moved into position to breach the front door, only the lead man reported that it had already been forcibly opened.

By the time Reilly and his men entered the tong, sweat had bubbled on his forehead, and salty streams seeped into the collar of his shirt. The Kevlar vest he had on didn't help matters, but what really hit him hard, enough to stop him in his tracks, was the thick, metallic scent in the air.

Reilly had found the red sticky to go with the red hot.

Two feet into the tong lay a headless man. Reilly sidestepped the crimson pool that had poured from the severed neck. The edges had already coagulated into a gel dam, preventing further spreading. He thought of searching the man for identification but changed his mind. He'd have to step into the sticky to get close enough. He stood and shook his head at the splatter that had sprayed the whitewashed walls. *What the hell happened here?*

The tactical team on the upper floors shouted *Clear!* faster than expected. That told him one thing—no resistance. *More bodies, I imagine.*

He was right.

What he had originally thought was the buzzing of an electrical current turned out to be an assault by another group of misfits associated with death: flies. Reilly let out a breath and turned to the bottom of the bloodstained stairs. *Lead the way, my buzzing friends.*

After passing the second decapitated man, he gave up trying to avoid the blood. It's like walking in mud; eventually, you say, "Screw it," and give in, because what's the point? The entire shoe would need cleaning.

Reilly had seen a lot during his twenty years with the Bureau. Death didn't bother him, but headless humans did. He had counted nine so far—more than enough to make him shiver under his weighted vest.

He never understood the thought process behind choosing decapitation over the simplicity of a gun. A firearm provided distance. Decapitation was close and personal. All he could conclude was that a person who reveled in this manner of dispatching people put absolutely no value on life. How could they? It's traumatic to see the aftermath, let alone watch it take place. Reilly couldn't imagine being the executioner.

He continued up the stairs as he heard the assault team's stomping boots make their way toward him. The top floor had been cleared.

"No threats," said the team leader as he came into view. "Our job here is done. I'll leave six men outside the building until SFPD can set up a contained perimeter."

Reilly nodded.

The team leader took another step but stopped and grabbed Reilly by the arm. "It's bad in there." He motioned to what remained of a shattered door barely hanging by its hinges.

Reilly's intelligence indicated that the top floor was where Jing Woo held court. From the look on the team leader's face, Reilly had a pretty good idea that questioning the elusive leader would be a no-go. He stepped through the doorway, careful not to spear his arm on a splinter.

The room was still lit, by his count, with fifteen candles of varying heights. He didn't see the body right away, his eyes needing a moment to adjust to the lower light levels. But once they did, it was unavoidable.

Lying on top of a small teak table, in the middle of the room was Jing. His head, both arms, and both legs from the knees down hung off the edges. The flaps of his robe lay open, revealing his grisly death. He had been opened from sternum to pubic bone.

Reilly took a step forward, unsure whether the shadows from the candle lighting were deceiving his eyes. They weren't. Jing had been gutted. Only an empty cavity remained. Careful of where he stepped, Reilly moved around to the other side of the table where he discovered Jing's innards, completely intact and left to rot.

Later, when medical examiner Timothy Green weighed in, he said, "He was alive when his organs were removed. While the procedure was speedy and precise, I believe he felt every bit of it." Green also reported high levels of amphetamines in Jing's body. "Most likely used to keep him from passing out during the procedure."

It was obvious to Reilly that someone else had wanted

Jing more than he had. Was it to punish Jing for the disorder that had taken place on his watch? Had they wanted to silence him? Who knew? This was a first for law enforcement in San Francisco. Never had the walls of Chinatown been breached. The department had moved into uncharted waters, and no one knew what to expect from the vacuum created by Jing's death. All they could do was hope for the best.

Chapter 2

My head felt clear, and my thigh was near full recovery. What more did I need—a doctor's note? Apparently. I couldn't get a word in without my supervisor, Special Agent Reilly, cutting me off. Technically, I was still on paid medical leave. It had been two weeks since the raid on the Hop Sing Tong and things had quieted down. So I thought.

"I don't want to hear it, Abby."

"But—"

"I told you to take the entire week off—not a few days."

"Yeah, but—"

"I can't believe you actually came in."

"It's important."

"And by the way, what's this I hear about you not wanting the promotion? Who turns down a promotion?"

I folded my arms across my chest and leaned back in my chair. My mouth had officially gone on strike. If he wanted an answer, he would first have to hear me out.

We sat in silence. Daggers flew forth from our eyes… well, from mine. Neither side was willing to give in.

Character weakness was not an attribute agents coveted. In the end, Reilly folded. I sure as hell wasn't going to.

"Fine, what's so important that you had to come to the office to tell me?"

I removed my laptop from my shoulder bag and placed it on his desk. "It's not over."

I was fresh off the Cotton Candy Killer case, a husband and wife's tour of San Francisco that involved killing people and creating crime scenes utilizing their body parts in a scenario that tied back to something famous about the city.

I had teamed up with Kyle Kang, a detective with the San Francisco Police department, to work the case. We'd eventually caught up with the killers, and their reign of terror had come to an abrupt end. Both of their bodies were at the morgue.

But while wrapping up the investigation, I realized there was more to the case than we had previously thought.

The Carlsons' laptop was full of pictures and videos of them committing the grisly murders. It also contained the online game "Chasing Chinatown" that had motivated their kills.

As they uploaded proof of their deeds, the Carlsons advanced in the game. It was clear someone else was involved, so after their death, Kang and I had assumed their identities and continued playing the game, even staging and photographing a fake murder scene in the hopes of uncovering the people behind it.

"What's not over?" Reilly scrunched an eye.

"The Carlson case. Chasing Chinatown is still in play."

"I don't understand. The Carlsons were the killers, and they're laying stiff on a table. Plus, we raided the Tong and Jing Woo, the man behind the game was—"

"Hold that thought. Hear me out. As you know, I uploaded the contents of the Carlson's laptop to my own hard drive to help with our investigation," I said as I clicked on the game application. "Detective Kang and I never did submit the photos from our staged crime, so I did it last night out of curiosity. The game congratulated me on completing the chase in San Francisco and gave me five more objectives to complete."

"Where?" Reilly asked.

I turned the laptop toward him. "Bangkok."

"Thailand? This game takes them around the world so they can kill people?"

"Pretty much. But that's not all. I also found this." I pulled up the leaderboard I had discovered. "They're not the only ones playing."

Reilly leaned in. "Are these all teams, like the Carlsons?"

"Yeah, there are twenty. Well, nineteen now. From what I can gather, they're running around the world and targeting innocent people based on the objectives the game gives them."

Reilly remained quiet. His eyes focused on the screen, and his mouth opened slightly. He hadn't been expecting that.

"It's live, too, you know," I said, breaking the silence.

His eyes met mine. "How do you know?"

"The map of the world shows where everyone is and their path of travel. Whenever a team completes an objective, or what the game calls an Attraction, it broadcasts it. Shortly after I submitted the photos of our crime to complete the last Attraction in San Francisco, a pop-up bubble appeared on the map stating that the Carlsons had completed the Chase in San Francisco."

Reilly leaned back in his chair and ran a hand through his hair. "This is beyond the Bureau, Abby. We're talking international, with nineteen killers—"

"Teams. There could be one, two, or more people in a team. We don't know."

"They're moving from city to city, from country to country. This is a logistical nightmare. The number of law enforcement agencies in each country—and let's not forget about Interpol—that would need to be briefed... Wait. Scratch that. First, they would need to be *convinced* that this game is real. Just coordinating all of that is a feat in itself."

"That's not all."

Reilly shifted in his seat. "Don't tell me you found something else."

"I don't think they'll be able to utilize the game to help

them. We have access to the Carlsons' account and that's it. We can share the information we have about the game and brief them on how to recognize a crime scene that might be connected to Chasing Chinatown, but other than that, they'll have a harder time stopping the murders than we did."

Reilly shook his head before letting out what sounded like a defeated breath. "Let me run this up the flagpole. I'll get back to you about the next steps."

"Speaking of next steps, I want it on the record that I'm not interested in being your spokesperson for the investigation."

"Are you kidding? You know more about this than anybody."

"You know just as much as I do. It's a waste of time for me to travel around briefing people."

"And what do you propose you'll do instead?"

"That I continue playing the game. In Bangkok."

Chapter 3

I left Reilly alone in his office to simmer with a double dose of the Monday blues. The logistics of notifying and briefing law enforcement agencies across the world wasn't something I wanted to be involved with. As much as the FBI had a responsibility to notify those countries, it wasn't our job to police and capture the killers. No matter what decision came down the pipeline, I had one goal in mind: to track the mastermind behind the game. I told Reilly that our focus should be nabbing the person responsible for the game and that *I* was the person best suited for that job.

I still hadn't had a chance to tell my unofficial partner, Detective Kyle Kang, about my latest revelation. I knew it would ruin his day as it had Reilly's, but last time I'd checked, I wasn't the Easter Bunny.

I tried his cell for the third time and again got voicemail. *Why aren't you picking up?* With a big sigh, I called the precinct and was transferred to his actual partner, Detective Pete Sokolov.

"Agent Kane. How can I help you?" Sokolov's Russian accent tended to fluctuate depending on his mood. Stress made it thicker and, to some degree, broke his English more than usual.

"I'm trying to track down your partner. Have you seen him?"

"Last time I see him was in hospital. You call his cell phone?"

"Yes, I've left two messages but haven't heard back."

I could hear Sokolov frowning through the phone. "Hmm, not sound like him. I will check his apartment."

"You know what, I'm heading in that direction. I'll stop by, but thanks for the offer."

"You tell me if you find him, okay?"

I told Sokolov I would. While my casework didn't rely on Kang's involvement, I wanted to continue working the case with him. He knew all the minute details about the game, the killers and the crime scenes. Plus, two heads were better than one. Once word got out about serial killers playing a global game á la the Amazing Race, there would be a lot of department heads around the world trying to coordinate their response. Translation: clusterfuck.

If I could steer Kang and me away from that, we could focus on the head of the snake: the game developer.

Kang lived in Russian Hill, a neighborhood famous for its crooked Lombard Street. I lived five minutes away in North Beach. Our proximity to each other helped with our partnership.

I parked, walked up the steps to his Victorian duplex and knocked. As I waited, I watched people walk their dogs, pick up coffee at the nearby convenience store, and catch the number 10 bus at the corner. He lived on a lively street; people were always out and about, the complete opposite of my sleepy enclave. I knocked once more, louder and longer, and resumed my people watching. After a moment or two, I took out my phone and dialed his cell once more. Voicemail. Again.

Dammit, Kyle. Where are you?

I knocked once more, but this time I threw in the doorbell I had just noticed. No sooner had the chimes quieted than I heard what I could describe only as a cackle coming from inside. The shrill voice grew louder, accompanied by the clacking of heels against a wooden floor. Something about the pitch, something familiar, bothered me. The laughter grew closer. It was only footsteps away from the front door when I heard a voice coo, "Stay put, Big Boy. I got it." Not in a breathy, sexy way but in a teenage, Japanese anime way.

Please don't let it be who I think—

Before I could finish my thought, the door swung open, and standing before me was the tall, thin, ivory-toned Suzi Zhang.

Her nauseous giggling stopped the moment she set eyes upon me. Instead of tightening the pink silk robe she was wearing, she put both hands against the doorframe and leaned forward, allowing her robe to flap open in the breeze and display the sparkly matching bra and panties she wore.

Her hair had been tossed into a bun on top of her head with a few tendrils framing her small, round face. Her makeup was perfect; I couldn't understand how, since I had a pretty good idea of what I had interrupted. And lastly, she towered over my five-foot-one frame thanks to the pair of black stripper heels she wore. I imagined they were permanently grafted to her feet.

I was momentarily embarrassed. I had interrupted Kyle during what was obviously a very private, and sadly, gross moment. But that didn't last long. *Who answers the door dressed in lingerie, heels, and a flimsy silk robe? Oh, I know, a tramp.*

Her smile turned into a smirk, and one of her eyebrows rose. "Oh, it's you."

I didn't want to let on that I found any of this surprising. I knew she wanted a reaction. "Is Detective Kang available?" I kept my tone neutral.

She used one of her manicured nails to scratch the corner of her mouth before flashing another plastic smile. "Kyle, your employee is here," she called out before turning and walking away.

Remain calm. She's just a bimbo.

A few seconds later, a robed Kang appeared. His cheeks were flushed red, and he did his best to avoid eye contact. He swallowed before speaking. "Abby, uh… hi. What are you doing here?"

"I should ask you the same thing. Shouldn't you be at

work?"

"Oh, I…uh, I took the day off."

"Mmm-hmmm."

"What do you mean, 'Mmm-hmmm'?"

"Look, I'm sorry I broke up your recovery efforts, but I have something important to discuss with you. It would be better if we didn't talk here."

A disheveled Kang met me at the La Boulange Bakery on Columbus Avenue thirty minutes later. No sooner had he sat down than his mouth spilled forth a series of apologies for not returning my calls, as well as for the awkward visit at his home.

I held up my hand. "I'm beyond that. Can *you* get past it?"

Kang nodded. "So what's this important information that you have to share?"

I removed my laptop from my shoulder bag and placed it on the table.

"Don't tell me—"

"I won't. I'll just show you."

Chapter 4

I refrained from saying any more than needed to walk Kang through my latest discovery in the Chasing Chinatown game.

He sat quietly across the table from me with his face resting in the palm of his hand. After a moment of reckoning, he lifted his head. His eyes were glassy. He let out a breath of air before a hint of a smile appeared on his face. "What are you thinking?"

That's the Kyle Kang I know.

"My supervisor is figuring out the best way to brief law enforcement in all those cities. I'll tell you now, I have no interest in becoming the poster child for the case and heading out on tour to help."

"That would suck."

"Our time would be better used in locating the guy behind the game. There'll be plenty of egomaniacs vying to be the one who locates and captures the killer in their city— a competition between the various agencies."

"Very much. I can see Rome bragging that they got their guy first or some crap like that." Kang drained the last of his coffee.

"The truth of the matter is, the only way to dismantle the game is to take down the person behind it. There are plenty of nut jobs out there willing to sign up and play."

"You want to keep playing the game?" Kang questioned.

"So long as we have access to the Carlson's account, we have to keep trying. It's the only way forward for us."

"One problem though:" Kang said, "Cavanaugh."

Captain Richard Cavanaugh was Kang's supervisor, and he hated that I had roped his detective further into a case that should have been closed. To lessen the politics and help Kang out, I'd had the bureau officially take over SFPD's part of the investigation to keep Cavanaugh from messing with it. The FBI had informed the rotund captain that I needed Detective Kang to help us indefinitely. Cavanaugh didn't have the balls or the political clout to fight us on it.

"The case is ongoing, and you're still helping the bureau. There's nothing he can do to stop you."

"Okay, problem solved, but I still don't understand how playing the game is an advantage for us. The San Francisco part of the game is finished. The next step is Bangkok. Wait. Tell me that's not what you're thinking."

I grinned at Kang. "Clear your schedule."

Chapter 5

Creep. Creep. I am the Creeper. Who will get lucky tonight?

The lone figure weaved his way through the mix of anxious men entering the small soi, a side street just off Sukhumvit Road, the main artery that ran through the middle of Bangkok. Even with the colorful neon lights casting a bright wash of dancing spotlights across the sidewalk and nearby buildings, he was almost invisible. Careful to move neither too fast nor too slowly, he avoided overtaking and made sure not to sidestep. To the crowd of tourists that surrounded him, he was never there.

He continued along the lively side street, his gait vanilla and his mind focused on finding a pretty prize for the night. He'd had many in the last few days, though none could give him the satisfaction he wanted and needed. He was on the verge of giving up on this location and trying another.

Which one of you pretties? Who will it be? The Creeper is here. Creep. Creep.

He passed one of the many sidewalk bars, eyeing his competition—loudmouth *farangs* drinking cheap Thai beer and listening to booming dance music. He watched them eagerly partake in the nightly courtship with half-naked women who gyrated for their attention.

Young and attractive, they would slither across laps, hug hairy arms, poke at doughy bellies, and dole out endless smiles and laughter. In return, the men would lavish these women with riches from the bar: a watered-down lady drink that earned the women a 40/60 split with the establishment. Here on the tiny strip, the farangs were kings and the barstools were their thrones.

The Creeper only sneered. Pathetic sex tourists with second-rate women were what he considered the bunch to be. He deserved better. He left the sidewalk and headed into Nana Plaza, where the go-go bars were. The dancers were the cream he craved.

It was nearing ten at night at the plaza. The best dancers were on stage, and almost every seat had a warm body occupying it. But not for long; it was pairing time. One by one, the men took the prettiest women off the shelf and back to their hotels or a nearby short-time hotel, though it wasn't always up to the man.

The women, especially the prettier ones, had complete control over who became a customer of theirs. As with any business, the women all sought the best men—those who weren't problematic and who had money to burn.

Some of the ladies hedged their bets on the best-looking farangs. Others opted for those whose pockets were stuffed with cash, and still a few held on to a strategy of finding the drunkest—one who would surely pass out the minute they got back to his hotel room. Of course, she would have requested payment up front.

The Creeper circled the first floor of the plaza, moving in and out of each bar. He was looking for the *one,* but nothing caught his eye. If he was disappointed, he showed no signs. He inhaled deeply. The city's humid night air had been soured with the scent of beer and heavy doses of cheap perfume.

Remaining optimistic, he climbed the stairs to the second floor and a half a dozen more bars offering more opportunities to find what he wanted. But the Creeper wouldn't need to look any farther than the bar to his left. From the corner of his eye, he caught sight of her—a glimpse, really, but her long, black locks against her creamy white back was enough to draw him into the club.

He entered, took a seat near the door, and ordered a beer from the server who appeared seconds later. He avoided eye contact and unnecessary conversation and instead focused on his prize.

Where did you go? You can't hide from the Creeper.

He scooted his chair against the wall so that his back was flush. He tucked his chin down and kept his bottle near his lips. He pulled his black baseball cap down farther, obstructing his face. Satisfied, his eyes went to work, shifting from side to side, searching. Halfway through his beer, he spotted her.

She had exited the dancers' room in the far corner, opposite where he sat, and was even more beautiful from the front. She wore a white bikini with matching pumps that made her appear to hop with each step. He glanced around the room. He wasn't the only one who had noticed the unattached beauty. The wolves were circling the lamb. He had to make his move, even if it risked drawing attention to him.

He set his beer down and walked straight toward her, intercepting her seconds before a drunken farang got to her. He quickly baited her with the promise of lady drinks, and she pounced.

He brought her back to his table near the door, sitting her down and shielding her from the many eyes that still bore through him to get to her. He ordered five lady drinks, knowing she would not drink more than one, but it sent a message. He wanted her.

He smiled. She smiled. He told her his name—Johan from Johannesburg. Not true, but it didn't matter because her reply was, "Ban from Bangkok."

"You come here often?" she asked.

He shook his head. "I prefer Soi Cowboy, but I was in the neighborhood."

"I work Soi Cowboy, at Shark bar, but I come here to see if better. I try this bar for a couple nights."

Lucky you.

They continued with small talk for another twenty minutes. She had already made a pretty penny off him from the lady drinks, but he made sure she knew more could be made if they closed a deal. "Whatever your price," he said, testing her willingness.

Was it enough to convince her? He couldn't be sure; her eyes were still wandering. She had a choice, unlike the other women who didn't quite have her looks. He engaged in more conversation and gentle thigh-rubbing. He focused on making her laugh. He told her how beautiful she was and got no response.

Stupid! She is told that a million times every night.

His conversation had to be original, clever at best. He had to entertain. There was no guarantee, yet he knew he had to have her. She was the one who could satisfy his desire, and the game.

Creep with me, Ban. You won't regret it.

Chapter 6

Ban woke the next morning, surprised to find that she was still in her date's bed. She rarely stayed the night, even if they paid for it and expected a second pop in the morning. But she had this time, not because this one was nice or because he was great in bed or because she was feeling lazy. She had stayed the night because a rope tightly secured her wrists and ankles to the bed frame.

How could I have been so careless? Over and over she replayed the events from the night before, looking for the mistake she was so sure she had never made. Ban had been in the game for close to four years—a seasoned pro. She had learned from others and from her own past mistakes on how to handle these men. She had a strict set of rules that she never wavered from. The most important were followed by almost all of the girls.

Rule One: Never finish a lady drink. She abided by that rule and never broke it, no matter how many drinks were bought for her, not even the ten that her one and only date of the night had purchased for her. She drank from a glass that she had personally taken from the hostess herself. No chance of it being spiked. She had all her faculties, as usual, never drinking more than a few sips.

Rule Two: Never, ever settle. Ban always got her asking price. Always.

Rule Three: Take charge of the situation. Control meant power, and power ensured safety. She always determined what they did and for how long. And last night, she did just that. She remembered everything from start to finish. He lasted for thirty seconds.

Rule Four: Condom. Condom. Condom.

Rule Five: Never accept any food or drink. Some devious men were known to drug their dates once behind closed doors. No matter how thirsty, no matter how hungry, a 7/11 was always a short walk away.

Rule Six: Leave the second they fall asleep. And they always did right after they had spent themselves.

But this time, things hadn't happened as planned.

Ban struggled against the bindings that held her in place. They were tied tightly, and not a chance of slipping free of them existed. Her eyes canvassed the bedroom. The one window had thick curtains covering it, and she assumed it was shut tight.

She remembered how he had surprised her at the last minute when they had arrived at the old condo building. Ban never went to them unless it was with a regular.

"I'm sorry, dear. I thought I was clear that I lived in Bangkok and had a condo," he said as he pressed his hand against the small of her back, ushering her forward.

Liar! She had no problem entertaining in serviced apartments or some of the new luxury condominiums that had been erected in the last three years, mostly because the men who stayed there were in Thailand on business, and their companies footed the bill. Almost every single one of them had a wife and kids back home. The odds of any of them being a psychopath fell on the minute side.

Those buildings were also equipped with CCTV cameras in the lobby, elevators and hallways. There were guards posted around the clock, and she actually had to leave her ID at the front desk in some of the buildings. She felt relatively safe in those well-appointed dwellings. But the older condos, well, any person could rent them, and there would be no way of proving that Ban had ever been there—the perfect variables for making someone disappear.

That aside, what really bothered Ban were the walls of the bedroom. They were lined with gray foam padding. It resembled large egg cartons and appeared to have been crudely stapled to the walls, while she was asleep. She swore it hadn't been there last night.

A loud bump at the door caught Ban's attention, then the sound of something hard scratching against the wood had her focusing. The sound wasn't fast and repetitive but slow and drawn out. It dragged the length of the door.

A beat later, the door swung open. There he was, her date. He was nude except for a white thong. Hers. It barely contained him. His scrotum spilled out from both sides of the strained material.

He smiled as he shut the door behind him. He was knock-kneed, and the top of his wrists rested on his hips, as he puffed out his chest and pranced around the room delivering a bad Mick Jagger impersonation.

"Hello, my pretty. Did you sleep well?" he asked.

Ban's thoughts were focused on how to escape, but first she had to regain control of the situation. "My arms hurt," she cooed. "Can you release me? I want to play with you again."

She was well aware of how vulnerable she was—nude and tied up. She tried her best to produce a sexy pose, but given her lack of mobility, struggled. She pouted and blinked her eyes, but it appeared to have no effect on the man who had grown content with watching himself in the mirror that sat on top of the dresser.

"Baby," she called out.

He ignored her, walked over to a small table tucked away in the corner of the room and switched on a portable stereo. Suddenly the room filled with music, rock music, the type that most associate with noise. It was loud but not loud enough to annoy a neighbor. Ban felt her heart beat faster. She worried. What if this weren't a game? What if she could not sweet-talk her way out of the situation? What if she had made a terrible mistake by saying yes when she should have said no?

She watched as he emptied the contents of a brown

paper bag he had brought into the room with him: a plate and some sort of square metal instrument. She realized it was a multi-grater when he waved it at her.

"Untie me baby. Let me take care of you," she tried once more.

He moved toward her, smiling but refraining from answering. He sat on the edge of the bed, near her legs. He put the plate down next to her and then pointed at the gray foam on the walls. "No one will hear."

Hear what?

She watched him lay his hand against her shin and grip it gently. Her skin tightened immediately as she tried to jerk her leg away.

"Shhhhhh, don't be scared."

He closed his eyes and inhaled deeply as he guided his hand higher. The rough, dry skin of his palm scratched at her. When he reached the inside of her upper thigh, he used his index finger to trace tiny circles. His touch sent chills through her body—chills that were more likely to induce vomiting than sexual pleasure.

She wanted to pull away, to shake his violating paw off her, but instead, she held still. She wondered, if only for a second, if this was another sexual quirk of his. Would he get off soon? She continued to feign interest in hopes of a satisfying him quickly and securing her own release.

She forced another smile only to watch his disappear. He grasped a handful of her soft flesh, kneading it slowly between his fingers. She let out a moan and thrust her hips gently, all while screaming for help inside. She did her best to remain calm for fear that he would hear her rapid heartbeats. She oozed sexuality but struggled to hold back the tears. Ban prayed for control. She prayed for the strength to get through this. She told herself over and over, *Make him happy. Get him off. Leave.*

But Ban could no longer contain herself. A tear broke free and ran down the side of her cheek. Her bottom lip started quivering uncontrollably. The knocking of her heart thumped louder. Surely he could hear it over the music.

Hold it together, Ban. She couldn't. He was no ordinary customer. He had gained control.

He released her thigh and picked up the grater. She watched as he placed it on top of her right thigh.

"Nooo," she mouthed, moving her head back and forth for clarity.

The teeth of the appliance gripped her skin and tugged on it a bit.

"Please. I beg." Ban pleaded once more, only to have her words go unnoticed.

"I like green papaya salad. *Som tum,* isn't that what it's called here?" He slid his tongue across the bottom of his lip before sucking it back into his mouth. "This might hurt," he whispered before closing his eyes and drawing a big breath.

Chapter 7

Reilly had heard back from the higher-ups and, surprisingly, they didn't want to expend too much manpower for the briefing. He was told that the Bureau's time would be better served focusing on the problems of our own country. There was plenty of crime fighting to be done in the good old U.S. of A.

"What does that mean?" I asked.

"It means we keep the brief simple. We send everyone the information we have and grant them an hour-long web conference to answer any questions. They're on their own after that."

"What about the mastermind of the game?"

"As far as my superiors are concerned, he's not a concern. They think everyone should focus on nabbing the players. The mastermind, in their heads, is an unknown. They said the evidence you've uncovered, while promising, wasn't enough to convince them that one exists."

"Promising? What the hell does that mean? Look, if this guy found twenty psychopaths to play his game, surely he can find twenty more. Taking out the players doesn't solve the problem."

"Abby…"

"I'm supposed to just drop it. File it away like it's not important."

"Abby!" Reilly raised his voice. "I didn't say that and I agree with you."

"Huh?"

"I went to bat for you." A smile stretched across Reilly's face. "I know you want to continue playing the game, and the only way to do that is to go to Bangkok. They were against it. They didn't want some rogue agent causing havoc in another country, but I convinced them we could trust you."

I swallowed. "Of course you can."

"I'm going out on a limb here. Don't make me look bad."

"I won't so long as there are no idiotic provisions attached to this."

"You need Bangkok's okay on it. As soon as you pull the materials together, I'll get them briefed and broach the subject of you working alongside their personnel."

"You know me. I can't be handcuffed, and I'm not running every move I make by someone over there. I can't work that way."

"I know, but let's just see if they're open to the idea first."

"Will there be any other agencies involved? CIA?"

"Not yet. We have one of our own embedded in the

American embassy. He'll be your liaison."

"You mean the guy who's supposed to keep an eye on me."

"If you want to call it that, yes."

"I don't need a babysitter."

"Then don't make a lot of noise while you're there."

I spent the rest of the day and most of the following putting together a presentation deck with all the information we had collected, along with a few helpful tips for catching the killers. Our hope was that the respective law enforcement would catch the game's participants in their city before they completed their Attractions and moved on.

Chapter 8

Songwut Soppipat, known since birth as Artie, weaved his way through the crowded sidewalk along Sukhumvit Road. With a bevy of food carts and merchants occupying the majority of the concrete path, foot traffic had been relegated to a narrow middle lane where Thais bumped shoulders and shuffled along, avoiding the occasional motorbike and stray dog. The sidewalks of Thailand were storefronts for the many entrepreneurs who rolled their portable businesses on and off the highly sought-after real estate on a daily basis. Only tourists found the lack of walking space annoying.

Artie had developed a daily routine that he worked hard to maintain, even in a job as unpredictable as his: a detective for the Royal Thai Police where he had worked for almost eleven years and showed no signs of slowing down.

He was assigned to the Thong Lo station that oversaw the Watthana district. That meant the station was responsible for policing the popular Sukhumvit strip of road that included the famous Nana Plaza and Soi Cowboy attractions, as well as numerous massage parlors. Artie rarely bothered with the petty crime and disorder that took place in those areas, preferring to focus on homicides.

He was light on his feet and looking forward to celebrating a case that he had closed that morning. A woman's body had been discovered inside a large suitcase floating in one of the many canals that snaked its way through the city. It was a case of a jealous boyfriend who had taken an argument too far.

His destination was a tiny street-side food cart near the entrance of soi thirty-eight. Artie had been eating at the makeshift restaurant almost daily for the last three or four years. As far as he was concerned, the owner, Pik, made the best food on the block.

"*Sawadee ka,*" the elderly woman called out as she saw Artie's familiar face appear in the distance. She maneuvered her stout frame around the food cart that also doubled as her kitchen to quickly clear one of the four tables of its dirty dishes. She motioned for Artie to take a seat on a semi-sturdy plastic stool whose legs had been worn down at least an inch and which had never met a wet cloth, much less disinfectant.

"*Sawadee kup,*" he replied with a smile that seemed to stretch for days.

"The usual?" Pik asked before returning to her spot behind the cart.

Artie nodded and reached for an unopened bottle of water that sat on the table. A few seconds later, one of Pik's helpers placed a metal cup filled with ice next to him. Artie poured the water into the cup and gulped it down faster than it could cool.

Midway through his two favorite dishes—som tum and grilled pork—Artie got the call, the one that would ruin his mood and his lunch.

Chapter 9

"Human som tum," the woman in the lab coat said without emotion.

Artie thought he must have heard her wrong. "Tip, are you saying someone made som tum out of human flesh?"

"Not my choice of ingredient, but yes," Dr. Tippawan Pradchaphet said, pressing more modeling clay into the partial human skull she was rebuilding at the black table against the wall. The platinum bangles on her left wrist jingled softly as she smoothed the transition from bone to clay. Reconstruction was one of her specialties.

Artie and Tip had history. They had dated briefly before realizing they were better off as friends. She was a forensic scientist and worked for the Ministry of Justice. Despite her departments chronic underfunding and the obvious age of her equipment, she was deadly accurate in her findings.

Between her skill and her unconventional appearance, she was a favorite with the media and the public. No other medical examiner in Thailand dressed in haute couture under their white lab coats or sported smoky-eye makeup.

Artie looked again at the bloody contents in the see-through bag that Tip had placed in a metal bowl on the lab table. Her familiar perfume teased his nose—she must have given herself a fresh spray before he arrived—but he tried to ignore the scent and maintain a professional front. She had a habit of trying to tempt him back into her arms, even though she was fully aware that as a couple, they were terrible. But it was a game she enjoyed playing with him.

She pointed at the sealed bag with her Swarovski-studded fingernail. "Take a closer look."

Artie picked up a metal tweezers and poked at the bag. "You sure about this?"

Tip let out a loud breath of air and tilted her head. Her crinkled brow conveyed all Artie needed to know: She was finished repeating herself. If she said it was human, it was human. But the real question was burning in his mind: *Who got turned into som tum?*

"You think there's a body lying around someplace?" he asked.

"Hard to tell. A few shavings off a limb wouldn't kill a person. Maim? Perhaps. Unless there's more of this special recipe elsewhere, the owner could still be alive." She looked at Artie flatly and shrugged her shoulders.

He rested both hands on his hips. "Tip, why is your department involved in something like this? Determining whether the flesh was human or not could have been done by a number of labs across Bangkok. It doesn't seem like the usual Tip case." Artie emphasized her name with air quotes.

"It's human som tum," she said, setting the cranium reconstruction aside. "It'll look good on the resume."

"You never let up on the blatant self-promotion do you?"

"Nope. And you could be a lot further in your career had you learned to toot your own horn a little." Tip followed her remark with a smile to let Artie know it was the truth, but a constructive truth. She had always been Artie's biggest supporter and had constantly bugged him— she described it as encouraging—to champion his own achievements, but that wasn't Artie's style.

"So is this officially your case?" she asked before tossing the bag of remains back into a refrigerated storage unit and padlocking it.

"It is now. The station chief called me personally to ask me to take over the investigation when the officer at the scene saw that it wasn't green papaya but some sort of raw meat. Is that why it was sent to you, for analysis?"

"No, it was already identified as human flesh by another lab, but I was brought on to confirm the results."

"Ah, the Tip stamp of approval."

"You got that right. Any leads yet?"

"You were my first stop after being briefed. The only other thing that was made clear to me was that the Ministry of Tourism wants to keep the case under the radar. If they had their way, it would be buried. Their biggest nightmare is that someone turned a tourist into som tum. Not exactly a selling point for coming to Thailand."

"Typical bullshit." Tip turned on her heel and headed toward the exit.

Artie followed. "Anything else you can tell me?"

She pulled the door open for him. "Not at the moment. I'll let you know if I discover anything else." She paused. "Drinks later tonight?"

Another temptation. Artie politely declined. He had an impossible case to solve, and drinking cocktails with his ex wasn't exactly the best way to start.

Chapter 10

Later that evening, Artie paid the crime scene a visit. He was intent on questioning the young lady who had made the grisly discovery. She was the manager of a massage shop located on soi twenty-two, just off Sukhumvit. He hoped she had something helpful to add to what he already knew.

"I came to work early on Wednesday morning to prepare an offering for Buddha," she said.

"And that's when you saw the dish?"

"Yes. I saw a plate of food and wondered who'd left it. When I took a closer look, I realized it was raw, shredded meat. At first, I got angry thinking someone had played a joke on me. But then I noticed the blood, and I realized something wasn't right."

"And that's when you called the police?"

She nodded. Artie prodded her a bit more, but she had no other information to offer up. He thanked her for her time and exited the shop. He stood on the sidewalk and looked around. Across the street was the Queens Park Plaza, an area made up of fifteen or twenty small bars. It was also home to a number of bar girls plying their wares. He had built a trusting relationship with one girl in particular.

Lucky had worked at the open-air bar near the entrance of the plaza for the last three years and was considered a veteran amid the constant churn of women trying their luck in the profession. Though most of the women in the plaza had seen better days, Lucky was a bright spot: only thirty years old with a flat stomach and a reasonable command of the English language.

Artie spied her sitting at the front of the bar, her eyes following the action up and down the soi. She wore a black dress with matching heels.

Lucky noticed Artie right about the same time. She knew what a visit by the detective meant. She moved nonchalantly away from her bar stool to the edge of the bar, away from prying ears.

"Hi, Lucky. How's business?"

"Quiet now. Low season. I think next month it will pick up. Why? You want to go short time with me?" She giggled and playfully poked Artie in the chest.

"I don't think I could handle you," he joked back.

Lucky lowered her voice and relaxed her smile. "Artie, why you visit me? What do you need?"

"Did you hear about what happened across the street, outside the massage shop?" He motioned with his head while he waited for a response.

"I hear. What type of person does that?"

"That's what I'm trying to find out. Did you see

anything unusual last night?"

"Like what? I see many unusual things every night."

"Did you see anyone hanging around the Buddha shrine?"

Lucky looked off to the side as she thought about Artie's question. "You know, I saw a farang looking at it last night. But what is strange about that? Many farangs like to look and take picture of the little shrines around the city."

"Can you tell me what he looked like?"

"He looked like a farang." Lucky's eyebrows dipped. "A white man," she continued. "Brown hair. Not tall. Normal size. No belly."

Artie knew he would need more to even begin to know whom he was looking for. "What was he wearing?"

Lucky pondered for a moment. "Jeans… a dark shirt. That's all I remember. I wasn't paying attention. I had a customer talking to me."

Artie wasn't making much progress. His leads were few. If Lucky couldn't give him anything substantial, he could see the case turning cold fast. *Not an option.* "Thanks for your time, my friend." He slipped her two hundred baht, as he always did after their conversations.

Just as he turned to leave, she grabbed him by his arm and squeezed. "Wait, I remember something."

"What? Tell me."

"The man had a handicap."

"You mean he was in a wheelchair?"

"No, he had a limp."

Chapter 11

It had been a few days since I had started briefing law enforcement in the cities that appeared on the Chasing Chinatown leaderboard. I had just wrapped up a teleconference call with Interpol and the Italian State Police in Milan. The ISP had been able to connect two murders that had taken place in the last three weeks with the game. Both of the victims were children—already disturbing—but when they described the crime scene, it got worse.

A small boy had been discovered in a storefront window of an empty retail space. He had been dressed in Versace and had been skewered on a metal rod to prop him up like a mannequin. My stomach had tightened as the inspector rattled off the details. I couldn't help but think of my own two children. What would I have done had that happened to Lucy or Ryan?

I thought of the parents and what they must have felt when they heard the news of their son's death. At first, it made me sick. Then anger set in. I wanted to catch the next flight to Milan and work the case. I wanted to catch the son of a bitch who had done that. I wanted to take a metal rod, shove it up his ass and ask him how he liked it. While I was busy fuming and plotting revenge for the little boy, Reilly stuck his head into the conference room.

"Got a minute?"

"Sure," I said as I shut my laptop and spun around in my chair, my face still tight.

He took a seat opposite me. "How are the briefings coming along?"

"Fine. It's a struggle in the beginning when I mention the game, but once I walk them through our case and the connection to the game, it gets easier."

Reilly clasped his hands together. "Abby, I'm having Tracy House finish the briefings. She's familiar with the details and can take over."

"Why?" I demanded, wondering what I had done wrong. House was the agent who had initially started the investigation that led to the capture of the Carlsons. She was also a friend.

"I just heard back from our agent in Bangkok. You and your detective friend are a go. I want you out there ASAP. Catch the a-hole behind this game, Abby."

The news about Bangkok, while great, had caught me off guard. My emotions were still in a twist from the Milan briefing. I had been so focused on the death of the Italian boy that I had lost sight of the big picture: To prevent more unnecessary deaths, the mastermind had to be caught and the game shut down. It was time to get my feelings under control and refocus on my mission. Reilly had pulled the trigger on the starting gun, and I exploded out of the blocks.

I put a call into Kang right away and told him we were a go. I wanted to leave for Bangkok as soon as possible, which meant he needed to get his affairs in order. I had my own responsibilities I needed to square away before leaving. Mainly, I had to tell my family that I would need to head out of town for a case. That meant my mother-in-law, Po Po, would be taking on the head-of-the-household duties. I wasn't looking forward to that conversation.

Lucy, my youngest at age six, always took my absence the hardest. "Why, Mommy?" she asked over dinner later that day. I always tried to break bad news to the family while we were eating. Somehow I thought food lessened the impact, though I wasn't sure how much it helped.

"There's a bad man in Bangkok who is hurting people. Mommy is going there to make him stop."

"When are you going to come home?"

"I don't know yet, but I'll call you every day, okay?"

"You come home soon, okay?"

She got out of her chair and walked over to where I sat. I lifted her onto my lap. "I will, sweetie. I promise."

"What did this guy do?" Ryan had grown increasingly interested in my work. Sharing the details was something I struggled with. Withhold information to protect him, or tell him the truth? More and more, I sided with the latter, and not just with him, but with all of them—though I tended to sterilize my feedback when Po Po and Lucy were present.

"Well, this guy created a game that encourages the players to hurt other people."

"Why did he do that?" Ryan had lowered his fork and stopped chewing for a second.

"Well, he's a bad guy. They do bad things."

"Why Bangkok police don't catch this guy?" Po Po chimed in.

"I'll be working alongside them."

Po Po shook her head as she stood to clear the table, starting with her and Lucy's plate. Ryan and I had taken seconds, as usual.

"Still not make any sense for you to go."

Po Po never shied from letting me know how much she disapproved of my out-of-town work. Her remarks made it perfectly clear. The responsibility of looking after Ryan and Lucy completely fell on her hands—something that ratcheted up my guilt meter to no end. It's not that she minded, but as she had pointed out in the past, I was their mother. I had signed up for the responsibility when I married my late husband and adopted the kids as my own.

"Up to you," Po Po muttered as she headed to the kitchen.

Recently, she had taken to stating that phrase when she didn't like something I did or if I disagreed with her. I wasn't quite sure what she meant by it. Was she saying the trip out of town had been my decision? Was she insinuating that if I somehow went ahead with this trip that I only thought of her as the in-house babysitter? I didn't. We'd had many discussions over that matter, but my actions always seemed to end up contradicting what I said.

I'm sure I read into it way more than I needed to. For all I know, she probably didn't even understand what she had said but liked the way it sounded. I'd like to think her comment was innocent, but I knew my mother-in-law and her passive-aggressive ways better than she liked to admit.

A few hours later, I had tucked both children into bed and said goodnight to Po Po before retiring to my room. I had just started my nightly bedtime routine of washing and moisturizing my face and brushing my shoulder-length black hair when I heard the opening introduction from the nightly news blare out from the small flat screen in my room. The anchorman made a big deal about welcoming a new anchorwoman to the show. With my head half in the sink, I wasn't really paying attention to the fanfare until a familiar voice caught my attention.

My eyes shot up to the mirror. Half of my face remained covered in thick white goo. I switched off the faucet and hurried out of the bathroom so I could see the TV screen, and I kid you not, staring straight at me was the dreaded dragon woman—Suzi Zhang. Her plastic smile, wider than a nose of a hammerhead shark, gave way to her perfectly paid-for row of veneers.

"Thanks, Jack. Good evening San Francisco. I'm so happy to be back in the Bay Area and able to rejoin my family here at KTVU. Many of you remember me from the morning news before I left for sunny Orlando. Well, I've returned, and let me just say, I missed this wonderful city and its people."

As she continued to blather about how wonderful everything was, all I could think about was how unfair things were right at that moment. It seemed as though that woman had infiltrated every part of my life. It was bad enough that I had to endure Kang's constant babbling about how wonderful she was, and of course, have to endure the occasional yet sickening run-in, but now she was part of my favorite news program, the one I fell asleep to most nights, drifting off to the calm and reassuring voice of the handsome and debonair Jack Archer.

And now that cackling she-devil ruined it. I would need to find another news channel. I couldn't stomach having to look at her nightly. And that pissed me off. *Why doesn't she go find some other news family?*

She went on and on about her stupid return, as if it had miraculously lifted the entire Bay Area out of a depression caused by her absence. *Did Orlando get sick of you and give you the boot?*

As I walked back to the bathroom, I swear her eyes followed me. It was like she knew I was listening and relished the opportunity to taunt me from my television set.

Chapter 12

Kang and I arrived at Suvarnabhumi International Airport two and a half days later. We deplaned the aircraft a little after midnight and found ourselves in a modern terminal awash with other recent arrivals sporting tired eyes. Apparently, a lot of international fights arrive in Bangkok from 11:00 p.m. to 2:00 a.m.

Reilly had already warned us that there would be no Thai congregation to meet us at the airport. Fine by me; I didn't need someone to hail us a cab and tell the driver what hotel we were staying at.

Rather than follow the crowd, Kang, of course, immediately went to a map on a wall to try to determine where we were and where we needed to go to pass through immigration and collect our luggage.

"Nuh-uh," I said. "Follow me." I then got in step with the others from our plane. A hundred-plus travelers can't all be heading in the wrong direction, right?

Getting lost wasn't something I wanted. I hadn't slept well on the plane, thanks to Kang's just-loud-enough-to-keep-me-up-but-not-the-others-around-us snoring. All I could think of at the time was falling face first on a clean bed. There's nothing quite like the perfectly short-lived sensation of cool sheets pressed against naked skin.

We were booked into the Landmark Plaza Hotel on Sukhumvit Road. The travel agent that handled my department's travel arrangements had said it was a central area and would make moving about the city easy. I had taken her word for it, but now I was rethinking things as the cab turned onto the main strip and started its slow crawl to our hotel.

The sidewalks were busy with groups of men and scantily clad women hanging on to them. Neon lights flashed above crowded bars that featured more of the same. Hawkers selling trinkets and food complemented the lively nighttime crowd.

Kang summed up my thoughts pretty well. "Are we staying in the red-light district?"

"Apparently."

While popular with tourists and business travelers, it turns out the Landmark was also within walking distance of Nana Plaza, what the front desk clerk would later tell us was a "fun and lively entertainment center."

After checking in, Kang Googled the place on his mobile. "Go-go bar central with a good mix of women and ladyboys."

"Ladyboys?"

"Yeah. They're men that dress like women, only these men really look like women, and most people can't really—

"

"I know what they are. I'm just surprised that this 'entertainment' plaza is in a largely touristic area." I then answered myself, realizing why a lot of men come to Thailand: sun and fun.

Kang's insistence that we step out and sample some readily available street food steered me away from heading up to my room. He didn't need to try very hard to deter me after he'd said the magic word: food. What can I say? I like to eat.

We left our bags with the front desk and stepped back out into the steamy night. Even though it was closing in on three in the morning, the heat was very apparent, and the humidity latched onto me creating a stickiness I knew I would have to live with the entire time we were in Thailand.

Looking up and down Sukhumvit, I spied a steady stream of partiers on both sides of the road. Kang led me past a bar on wheels parked on the sidewalk. In front of it were five bar stools, two occupied by women who were smiling at Kang as we passed. A large grin appeared on his face.

Apparently, one of the women saw that as an open invitation, grabbed his arm and pulled him toward her. He didn't appear to be putting up much of a fight. He must have forgotten about his girlfriend, Sushi, or whatever her stupid name was. Regardless, it was too good to pass up. I slowed my pace and hung back, giving the impression that we weren't together. *Let the show begin.*

Within seconds, she had locked her legs around Kang's torso, her grasp tight. Not that he fought it. She grabbed his hand and playfully entwined her fingers between his. He giggled like a shy boy who was about to get to first base for the very first time. *Men—they're so predictable.*

"What your name?" she asked with a heavy accent.

"Kyle," he said as he looked down, intimidated by the aggressive eye contact she delivered. He had completely forgotten about me. I hoped so, anyway; I sure as hell wouldn't have been embarrassing myself like that in front of a coworker, but I digress. *Back to the show.*

Within seconds, Kang had been reduced to a puppet willing to do the bidding of whatever that woman wanted. *Build me a house. Okay. Buy me that diamond bracelet. Okay. Take me on a trip. Okay. Support my entire extended family. Okay... Oh, Kyle, please don't make me save you from this situation.*

Her childlike questioning continued. "Where you from?"

"San Francisco."

"California," she cheered.

"That's right. Wow, you're smart."

Smart? Puh-lease. That's basic geography.

"You come for holiday or work?"

"I'm here for work."

Her grasp tightened. "How long you stay in Thailand?"

"I'm not sure."

She reached up to play with his chin and batted her eyelashes. "You buy me drink?"

"Uh, I'm not sure—"

"Why, baby? I not beautiful for you?"

"No, of course you're beautiful, very beautiful."

The show got more entertaining by the second. I had made myself comfortable on a low wall by then, delighted that Kang had insisted we get something to eat. I pulled out my phone and started snapping pictures should his memory falter and need a refresher.

Kang succumbed to her request for a drink, not even once turning to see if I had stuck around. She sipped the colored liquid in the rocks glass while her other hand played with the buttons on the front of his shirt. As much as I wanted to see how this show would play out, I couldn't ignore my rumbling stomach. I stood, ready to break up the party, when the unexpected happened.

The woman leaned in, and her voice dropped to a deep baritone. "You like ladyboy?"

The look on Kang's face was priceless. I swear he fought harder to escape her grasp then he had a few weeks ago when we were fighting our way out of the underground tunnels of Chinatown.

Laughter erupted from my mouth as I watched him swat her arms off of him and shimmy himself out of her now noticeably muscular thighs; her dress had ridden up in the struggle.

Tears poured from my eyes. My abs ached as I struggled to find a break in my uncontrollable wailing to catch my breath. I dropped to the ground on my hands and knees in a fit worthy of an Oscar for Best Laughing Performance. I snorted like a pig, batted my hand against my thigh. Heck, I think I may have even peed myself a little right there on the sidewalk. I had lost complete control, and I didn't care because I had not laughed that hard since, well, ever.

"Abby! Abby!"

I heard the words coming out of his mouth, but I couldn't stop. I looked up, glassy-eyed. A red-faced Kang stood over me.

"Seriously?" He reached down and tried to pick me up by my arm, but I was limp with laughter. Eventually, I composed myself long enough to get to my feet and walk crookedly away from the bar. "Oh my God," I gasped, trying to regain my breath. "Your face! 'You like ladyboy?'" I hung on his arm to keep my balance as I dissolved into laughter again.

Over our meal, he glared at me as he picked at his grilled squid. Apparently, my random fits of mouth-covered snorts between bites of my som tum had ruined his appetite.

After we parted for the night, I giggled myself to sleep. No matter what happened from that point on, that night had made the whole trip worth it. And it would continue to entertain for at least two more years.

Chapter 13

The next morning, I dragged myself out of bed slowly, thinking it felt like seconds ago that I had lain on my pillow. My wake-up call had come through on my cell. A woman's voice I didn't recognize and had trouble understanding started to have a conversation with me. I tried to clear the sleep from my head and follow what the woman was saying. "What?"

The person on the other end had a strong accent and ended every phrase by saying, "*Ka.*" I sat up, hoping it would help with deciphering her words. No such luck. It probably didn't help that I didn't have nearly enough sleep.

After multiple attempts to understand this woman, I finally heard some rustling on the other end of the line and then the clear and upbeat voice of a man.

"Agent Abby Kane?"

"Yes. Whom am I speaking to?"

"My name is Songwut Soppipat."

"What?" *Here we go again.*

"Detective Songwut Soppipat. But you can call me Artie. It's a lot easier."

"I'm sorry... Is it Detective Artie?"

"Yes, but you can lose the 'Detective.' Artie is fine."

"I'm usually not this difficult."

"It's not a problem. I'm sure your flight arrived late last night. They all do."

"It did. Thanks for understanding."

"I'm calling because I'll be your contact while you and your partner are here in Thailand. I'd like to meet as soon as possible, as I was just informed of your arrival earlier this morning. I'm eager to hear more about your intentions here."

After I hung up with the detective, I called Kang and told him we were sitting down with our Thai contact in an hour. I met up with him in the lobby a little later, and we proceeded to the Starbucks across the street from the hotel to wait for Artie.

"I'll get us something to drink," Kang said and moved toward the counter.

I looked for an empty table and sat. I was rummaging through my purse, looking for my tin of loose-leaf tea, when from the corner of my right eye I noticed that a man had appeared next to me.

"Agent Kane?" he asked softly.

"Yes, that's me." I looked up at a Thai man with a pleasant smile. I had expected the detective to be dressed in a suit; instead, he wore a white polo shirt and cargo pants and a holstered weapon sat on his hip out in the open. It made sense considering the conditions outside the air-conditioned coffee shop. He appeared fit and wore his hair tight on the side with an inch of gelled spikes on top.

"I'm Songwut Soppipat—Artie." He stuck out his hand.

I stood in an attempt to give him a proper greeting, but he quickly told me to sit. I shook his hand and returned a smile. I watched him pull up another chair, flip it around and take a seat.

"There are two of you, right?" he said. His eyes wandered.

"Yes. My partner, Detective Kyle Kang, he's with the San Francisco Police Department. See the tall guy getting coffee?" I motioned with my head. "Can I get you a cup?" I quickly offered.

He shook his head. "Thanks, but I had one earlier."

When Kang returned, I made the necessary introductions. The three of us then stared at each other for a moment before I took the lead.

"Artie, if you could tell us what you know, it would help me fill in the blanks without repeating things you've already heard."

Artie nodded and told us what he knew, which wasn't much. The way Reilly had spoke back at the Bureau, it sounded like the Royal Thai Police had been fully briefed.

All Artie knew was that we had come to Thailand on a hunch that a suspect in a murder investigation might be hiding out in Bangkok, and that we wanted to work alongside Thai authorities to determine if it were true.

"Well, there's a lot more to that story." I quickly brought Artie up to speed on Chasing Chinatown.

"Playing the game led you to Bangkok?" Artie asked, scrunching his brow.

"Not only that, we have reason to believe that someone is currently playing the game in Bangkok." I had brought my laptop with me to the shop but wasn't sure if it was the best place to reveal the game. I looked around and saw a table in the far back left-hand corner of the coffee shop, away from wandering eyes, and suggested we move.

Things clicked fast for Artie as I walked him through the screens: the cities, the Attractions, the leaderboard.

"And each Attraction requires they kill a person?"

"Pretty much," I said with a shrug. "Once the player cracks the riddle for each Attraction, they receive a task. It requires that they make a creative kill, one that ties into the spirit of said task, which we believe is always associated with something popular in the city. The player uploads a picture or video as proof to unlock the next Attraction."

"And once they've completed all of them, it unlocks a new city."

"Correct."

Artie leaned back and folded his arms across his chest.

His face tightened as the information I had fed him sunk in. I had seen this look before on the faces of those I'd previously briefed.

"So you're sure we have one of these individuals in Bangkok?"

I pulled up the leaderboard again. "According to the game, yes. What I can't tell you is if it's one person, a team, or more."

"This is the person or the persons you're after?"

"Your department was briefed earlier in the week about this situation and the possibility that a serial killer might be on the loose in Bangkok. I'm guessing you heard of no such thing."

Artie shook his head. "Sorry, I haven't. Bureaucracy," he offered. "So are you here to help us catch this person or persons?"

"Not necessarily. We're after the mastermind behind the game, but we believe our only shot at finding this person is to continue playing the game as Team Carlson—the killers we put an end to back in San Francisco. Their next destination was Bangkok."

Artie picked at his thumbnail for a moment before looking back at Kang and me. "You mentioned that the kills are usually tied into something that is representative of the city."

"That's right."

"Well, I think our killer has already struck."

Chapter 14

"Som tum?" I said, crinkling my brow.

"You probably know this dish by its other name: green papaya salad," Artie said.

It clicked. "Yup, I know that dish."

"Human som tum would be in line with the game play we've seen so far," Kang said. "Sounds like the Creeper is active."

"The Creeper?" Artie perked up.

"According to the leaderboard, that's the name of the individual or individuals playing the game in Bangkok: Team Creeper."

"You find the body yet?" I asked.

"Not yet, but the medical examiner said there's a chance the victim could still be alive. The amount of human flesh found in the dish wasn't enough to signify certain death."

"I guess the killer could be keeping his victims alive," I pondered. "The game doesn't necessarily call for a kill. But I think whoever offered up the flesh is probably dead."

Artie nodded in agreement. "I'm still a little confused on how we're supposed to go about catching this guy. Am I on my own now?"

"I've been thinking about that all morning," I said. "I think it's better if we work together. My hunch is that the Attractions are the same for all teams that come to Bangkok. So when we start playing the game, one of our tasks should be in line with the human som tum. The sooner we start, the faster we can catch up and hopefully nab Team Creeper."

"What about the mastermind?" Artie asked.

I shrugged. "All we can do is play the game, learn and hope that leads us to him."

Artie suggested we have a look at the crime scene while he continued to fill us in on his case. We piled into a cab and arrived at the Happy Time massage shop fifteen minutes later.

"This is soi twenty-two. It's a popular place for tourist, many hotels, bars, and massage shops."

He wasn't kidding. In the area where we exited the cab, I counted four small bars and five massage parlors.

Happy Time had floor-to-ceiling windows that occupied the storefront, giving us a clear view inside to the six oversized and very comfy chairs used for foot massages. Outside the shop sitting on plastic stools were five young women dressed in yellow polo shirts and black pants. They were doing their best to entice the passing men to come inside for an oil massage.

I turned to Kang with a coy smile on my face and

whispered, "Want to try your luck again?"

He only shook his head at me before looking away to observe the area. I stifled a giggle.

"This way," Artie motioned.

We followed him a few feet to the left of the shop. We stopped in front of a miniature, ornate temple on a pedestal. "This is a *san phra phum* or spirit house. You'll see them all over Thailand—outside office buildings and condos, near parks, inside stores, even in bars. Spirit houses show respect for the land. Thai people believe every place has a special spirit, and these little temples are like a shelter or gathering spot for them. Offerings are made daily to keep the spirits happy so they can grant wishes. Usually people make offerings in the form of flowers, candles, incense, and food."

"This is where the som tum was discovered?" I asked.

"Yes. The manager of the massage shop discovered it in the morning when she went to make an offering. It was a very disrespectful act to commit."

The little temple had been cleaned of the offense. Incense burned, and two opened bottles of juice with straws inside sat next to an orange and an apple. Yellow floral garlands big enough to fit around my wrist draped the two metal posts on either side of the tiny, wooden structure.

"Any witnesses?" I asked.

Artie nodded and pointed at a bar across the street. "Bar girls congregate there."

"Bar girls?" Kang inquired.

Artie shifted his gaze to Kang. "Girls that are there to entertain the customers."

"Oh, like hostesses."

"Yeah, except a customer can take them back to their hotel room."

"Ohhh," Kang nodded.

"I know one of them fairly well. If something goes down on this soi, she usually knows about it. I questioned her last night, and she said a farang—"

Artie noticed our puzzled faces. "—That's what we call foreigners or white people. Anyway, she saw one shuffling around the shrine the night before. She didn't pay too much attention because she had a customer, but she did say he walked with a limp."

"Is that all we have to go on?" I asked.

He nodded.

I took a deep breath and pushed it out. "Well then, if we're going to make any progress, we need to start playing the game."

Chapter 15

I knew how important it was to have Artie on our side and as close to us as possible. His expertise in Thai culture would help immensely when we had the task of deciphering the riddles and navigating the city. But more importantly, we needed him and a team of trusted men to watch our backs. I'm not big on group investigations, but in this case, it would be unavoidable; we needed to take precautions to protect ourselves in Bangkok just as we had in San Francisco: surveillance, muscle, the whole nine. We would need backup in case things went south. Even more so since we weren't operating on American soil.

"I assure you, I can organize an excellent team," he said. "You will be in capable hands."

If the bureaucracy that had kept Artie from even getting briefed appropriately was an indication of capability, I had my reservations. But what I didn't have was a lot of other options.

We returned to the Landmark Plaza and bunkered down in Kang's room. There I removed my laptop from my shoulder bag and fired up the game. As we waited for the introduction to play out, I summarized how we'd solved the last San Francisco Attraction to bring Artie up to date on how the riddles work.

"Make sense?" I asked.

"So the riddle will most likely tie into some sort of tourist attraction, either a place or an event, and that's where we'll get our clue to unlock the task. I get it."

I clicked on the first Attraction. An animation of a paper scroll unraveling appeared, revealing our first riddle.

Lie alongside the golden one, and you will find your destiny.

Kang and I were busy repeating the phrase in our heads when Artie brushed off the riddle with a dismissive hand gesture and blurted out the answer.

"This is easy. The riddle is talking about Wat Pho. It's the temple of the Reclining Buddha."

Kang and I looked at each other with surprise.

"Are you positive?" I asked, turning my gaze back to Artie.

"One hundred percent. Now what?"

"Well, if this is the right answer, which it probably is, our next step would be to visit this temple disguised as Team Carlson. It's what we've done so far."

"You don't think the people behind the game suspect anything?"

"Can't say for sure. Maybe, but we have no alternatives at the moment. All we can do is keep playing until we get shut down. At this point, it doesn't really matter whether they know or not."

Artie shifted in his chair. "That's a dangerous way to proceed." His tone was serious, and his eyes locked on mine.

"That's where you come in. We're hoping you can help alleviate those dangers."

Artie drew a deep breath as he leaned back on the wooden chair and fondled his chin while his other arm rested across his chest. He stared out the window for a moment, lost in his own thoughts. I wondered for a moment if he thought we were completely nuts. He finally turned his head back to us. "This will also endanger me and my men."

I nodded my acknowledgement. I wasn't sure if Artie was up to it. We still didn't know much about the detective, though he had proven himself useful so far. My concern, however, was whether he had the gumption and the ability to back us up.

"When do you want to visit Wat Pho?" he asked calmly.

I smiled a little. "As soon as possible."

Chapter 16

Artie surprised us when he suggested we hit the temple immediately. I thought he would need a day or so for logistics. No such thing.

"What's to figure out? You go to the temple. My men and I follow. You do what you need to do while we keep an eye out."

Artie needed only an hour to gather his men. We agreed to meet them at the Saphan Taksin dock. Kang and I were already dressed in our disguises when we spotted Artie. He had brought four other men with him and quickly made the introductions once we were together.

"They are good men. You can trust them with your life."

I hoped it wouldn't come to that.

The men looked the part, with their stern stares and squared-off jaws. That might impress a director casting for an action movie, but I was unmoved. An unusually tall man had a noticeable scar that ran down the side of his left cheek. He face showed no hint of emotion. They were all dressed in street clothes and wore either a light jacket or a sleeveless vest to conceal their weapons.

"This is the Chao Phraya River. It's a lot easier to get to the temple by water than by land," Artie said. He led us down wooden planks where we boarded a riverboat with an even mix of tourists and locals.

The boat was roughly one hundred ten feet long and fairly narrow and looked to hold about ninety to one hundred passengers. There were forward-facing rows of seating on either side of a middle aisle. Artie had secured a bench in the rear right side of the boat while his men created a buffer that prevented others from sitting where we were. It didn't take long before the boat propelled us out of the dock.

A cool breeze blew up off the river—a welcome relief for my slick face and neck. The weather app on my phone reported a current temperature of ninety-eight degrees with a heat index of one hundred six. I didn't doubt it.

I leaned back against the wooden bench, content to watch small fishing boats rock in the wakes created by our vessel as we sped by until Artie tapped me on the shoulder. He unfolded a piece of paper and flattened it on the bench, revealing a hand-drawn map of the temple, I supposed. Kang sat behind us but leaned over for a better look.

"This is Wat Pho. The large structure in the middle is where the Reclining Buddha is housed." He tapped at the drawing with a pencil. "There are two entrances on either side of the building. My men will position themselves here and here." He circled two areas. "There are a few blind spots so I'll enter the building with the two of you and remain nearby. Any questions?"

Artie had just simplified what would have been a fifteen-man, well-thought-out, FBI-driven operation to a sketched-out plan on a torn piece of paper. But it worked.

It took us fifteen minutes to reach our destination: Tha Tien dock. We debarked the boat with the other tourists and snaked our way up the plank to dry land. Straight ahead, I spotted gold spirals jutting up behind an enclosure wall.

Artie said a few words to his men, prompting them to break off from the group and disappear into the crowd. "The entrance to the grounds is just up ahead. I'll be right behind you," he said as he fell back.

"You ready?" Kang asked.

I put on a smile. "Of course, dear. Now let's go meet the golden one."

Kang and I paid our entrance fee and took a free map to the grounds. Inside the walls, the temple grounds were a lot larger than I had expected. The large structure that Artie had pointed out on the map made for an easy target to locate. Around it were smaller buildings, but we ignored those and followed the crowd to the main attraction.

Once inside the main temple, I faced a large golden Buddha literally lying on its side. It must have been close to two hundred feet long. As we moved in closer, I couldn't help but be distracted by the barrage of flashes bouncing off the smiling, bald man. I turned to Kang only to find him with his cell phone out, ripping off photos like a journalist in a war-torn country.

"What are you thinking?" he asked, finally pocketing his phone.

"Well, the riddle said to lie with the golden one, but clearly we can't get close enough to literally lie next to it." The statue was roped off, probably to prevent tourists from climbing on it for a photo. "It has to be something else."

"Do we really need to do this?"

"What do you mean?"

"Well, because of the human som tum, I'm guessing the task has to do with food."

"I hear you, but there are still too many variables. Is the task to do something with som tum or any Thai dish? Was leaving it on the shrine part of the task or part of the killer's creative expression? Plus, we need the right answer to the riddle to unlock the task."

Kang bounced his head from side to side. "You're right. Better to go through the motions and get it right the first time around." He looked around. "I wonder if we need to look for a contact like last time."

"Maybe." I scanned the crowd and spotted one of Artie's men standing near an entrance and studying a hand map for the grounds. The rest, including Artie, were incognito. I continued to search for an obvious clue to where we should go, but nothing jumped out at me.

Kang flipped open the Bangkok guidebook he had

picked up for the trip. "Maybe this will tell us something about the Buddha."

While he read, I scanned. That was when I spotted the clear, plastic bin against a wall. Inside I could see what looked like numerous Thai bills. *Hmmm, I wonder.* I walked over to the donation box, looking for a sign. I didn't readily see any. I deposited a twenty baht bill, about seventy cents USD, thinking maybe that might trigger something. Nothing. I looked back at Kang. He still had his nose buried between the pages. Probably didn't even realize I had walked away.

I had just started thinking that Artie might have gotten the riddle wrong when a thought entered my head. I hurried back to Kang. "Hey, I think we're being too literal with the riddle. Follow me."

We exited the large temple, not knowing if Artie and his men were behind us.

"Where are we headed?" Kang asked.

"There." I pointed at a gift shop a few yards away.

"Souvenirs?"

"Exactly."

We entered a small shop overstocked with countless knickknacks. I maneuvered around a family and through a tight aisle to where I saw a small table stacked with small replicas of the reclining Buddha. I picked one up and turned around to Kang. "I think we can lie with this one."

He smiled, and we proceeded to the cashier.

The young woman behind the counter took the statue and wrapped it in tissue. There were no other people in line, so I whispered the words, "Chasing Chinatown." She didn't acknowledge me but continued to wrap the Buddha. She then bagged it before typing a number on a calculator and showing it to me. I pulled out sixty baht, or about two USD, and handed it over. She then casually reached under the counter, removed a postcard, and slipped it into the bag before handing it to me.

I waited until we were out of the shop before removing the card. It had a glossy picture of a street lined with food vendors. "No surprises."

"What is it?" Kang asked.

I showed him the picture on the postcard. "I'm guessing the answer to the riddle is street food."

Chapter 17

Artie and his men appeared before us shortly after we had discovered the answer to the riddle. Neither Kang nor I saw their approach; knowing that made me feel much more comfortable with their abilities. The Thai detective was slowly proving his worth and earning my trust.

"What was in the gift shop?" he asked right away.

"The riddle asked us to lie with the golden one. It's impossible to lie next to the actual statue, but not this one," I said, showing him the little replica I had purchased. "We mentioned the name of the game to the cashier to trigger the gameplay, and in exchange, she gave us this postcard." I handed it to Artie.

"Street food?"

"That's what we're thinking. We'll have to key it in to be sure. If we're right, it'll unlock the task associated with this Attraction."

"Could also be soi thirty-eight. That's the actual street in the picture."

"We'll try both."

Artie looked over the top of my head, toward the gift shop. "Should we apprehend the cashier?"

"No, let her be. We're playing the game and need things to play out as they should."

Artie considered that for a moment before nodding his head in agreement. "All right. I know the owner of a nearby restaurant. We'll have privacy there and some good food. Follow me."

Artie led us out of the temple grounds and back to the dock, except this time we took a cross river ferry to the other side. From there, he led us through a maze of shops and food stalls in a nearby market until we reached a narrow lane with very little foot traffic. Toward the back of the lane, we entered a small restaurant with only a handful of diners. He pointed to a large table at the rear. "Go and sit. I'll order food for all of us."

When he returned, I had already unloaded my laptop and booted up the game. I motioned for Artie to sit beside me. "I want you to see how this works."

I clicked on the first Attraction, and the animated paper scroll appeared, revealing the riddle. Below that, in the answer field, I typed the words "Street food." A beat later the scroll unraveled further, revealing our task.

Serve up your favorite Thai delicacy on the streets of Bangkok.

Artie reacted first. "So that's the reason for the som tum."

"Basically the goal here is to envision the task creatively with a kill. Sickening, but that's the game."

"You mentioned earlier that you faked your last one. We'll do the same, right?"

"Yeah. After, we'll take some pictures and upload it to the game. That should get us access to the next Attraction."

Just then, a server arrived and placed plates of food on the table. Suddenly, nobody appeared to be hungry for the som tum, except Kang.

The young shop girl left the store shortly after providing the riddle to the couple. With her job completed, there was no need to remain there any longer. She was a deliverer, the one chosen to meet with the teams and give them their answer. When a team unlocked an Attraction in Bangkok, she received notification of who they were and prepared for their arrival.

Team Carlson was the second team to unlock Bangkok's first Attraction, which surprised her, because earlier in the week she had been notified of their disqualification from the game. After a quick call to the man who gave her orders, she was told to go ahead and provide them with the answer should they show up.

She hurried to a street corner where the motorbike taxis queued and hopped on the back of a bike. A few minutes of wind blowing in her hair and sitting sidesaddle, she arrived at her destination. After watching the motorbike drive off, she turned and headed into a nearby alley and then through a narrow doorway. She climbed five flights of wooden stairs, each one delivering its own unique creak. The stairwell was dimly lit, and the air smelled wet.

When she reached the top floor, slightly out of breath, she knocked on the first door to her left. Footsteps approached inside. A second later, the door opened enough for the slim woman to enter the one bedroom apartment.

Heavy curtains were drawn across the windows, but three lamps provided enough warm light for her to see the plump man sitting behind a desk and eating noodles from a bowl. She quickly brought her hands together in front of her chest and gave Somchai Neelapaijit a slight bow.

He didn't return the wai, but instead motioned with his fork for her to take a seat in a chair.

The woman spoke first. "Team Carlson was successful with their pickup."

Somchai slurped the last of his noodles into his mouth, chewed and swallowed. He wiped his mouth before speaking. "Same two people?"

"Yes, the FBI agent and the detective. They didn't suspect that anything was wrong."

"Good. And the other team?"

"He has yet to seek me out for the answer to the second riddle."

He thanked her for the information and dismissed her. When the door to the apartment closed behind her, Somchai turned to another man who sat quietly in the corner. "Find out why Team Creeper is stalling."

Chapter 18

Artie cut his men loose after our less-than-enthusiastic meal. The food, mostly Southern Thai cuisine, consisted of a variety of veggie and seafood curry dishes, which Kang continued to rave about long after our plates were cleared from the table. I was close to telling him to shut it but refrained.

Business in the small eatery had picked up, slowly eliminating our privacy, so the three of us headed back to the Landmark where we could formulate a plan for our next steps. Once there, we hunkered down in Kang's room again. He took the liberty of ordering a pot of coffee and hot water from room service.

Artie plopped down in a chair opposite me and repeated the task. "Serve up your favorite Thai delicacy on the streets of Bangkok." He thought for a moment. "So we make a dish with human parts?"

"We could," I said. "I don't think there is a right or wrong answer here. It's the entertainment factor. I suppose the goal is to surprise the creator of the game so as to gain access to the next Attraction."

"Would a copycat version work?"

I shrugged. "Best not to take chances."

Kang took a seat next to me. "What about human sausage? You know, mimic sai krok, those fermented sausages made from pork and rice. Good stuff." He gave us the thumbs up.

Ever since our arrival to the Big Mango, Kang had indulged in the offerings of every street food vendor we passed. It was nonstop. The guy ate everything in sight. I had initially tried to keep up, but the sheer amount of food he ingested was too much, even for someone like me. In fact, before heading into the hotel, he stopped once again at a vendor who sold deep-fried pork. I didn't see a pan for frying, so I assumed the food had been cooked elsewhere. I warned him. He brushed me off as though I were an overly concerned mother.

Back in Kang's room, the three of us continued brainstorming, looking for something that was simple and easy to fake. Eventually, we agreed on an unattended noodle cart that had balls of pork stacked inside a glass-enclosed shelving unit. Mixed in with them would be a pair of eyes.

"This seems doable. I have a contact who can lend us a noodle cart, and I have a friend who can provide us with a pair of fake eyes."

It was right around that time that Kang's stomach made a horrible whining noise that sent him hurrying to the bathroom, leaving Artie and I to laugh awkwardly. Kang's love affair with sidewalk food had suddenly turned into the relentless pursuit of always being in butt's reach of a toilet.

With him moaning on the commode and clearly not able to go anywhere for a while, Artie suggested the two of us look for a spot where we could plant the food cart. He already had a few places in mind.

"Best to leave him alone, anyway," Artie said, pressing the call button for the elevator. "There's nothing we can do."

I agreed.

We exited the hotel, and Artie flagged a cab. "I think I have a location that will work perfectly for this," he said as the cab pulled away. "It's on Sukhumvit, near soi twenty-three. The area is trafficked enough at night, so a discovery should be made fairly fast. We can follow up with our staged investigation and clear the cart shortly after. The faster the better."

"Why?" I asked.

"I don't plan on informing anyone but those involved. This is not something I want the Ministry of Tourism to find out about. They'll worry that the media will pick up on it and give them a PR problem." Artie took pause and then spoke again. "Will that be a problem? I mean, are pictures enough for proof, or do you need to show the investigation? We can if it's not a big spectacle."

I thought about what Artie said. I didn't think staging a fake investigation had helped our case in San Francisco.

Come to think of it, I didn't recall any of the crime scenes that the Carlsons staged ever being reported by the media. "I think all we need is to set up the cart and snap some pictures, so a location where we could do that without being bothered would be good."

"Are you sure? Maybe we should go through the motions, just in case."

"All right," I conceded with a nod. "If it's not a problem, it couldn't hurt."

Ten minutes later, our cab stopped near the Asoke BTS station just past a large intersection.

We walked another twenty feet along the busy road. A line of cars in gridlock as far as I could see waited patiently for their turn at the green light.

"This is the area I'm thinking about," Artie stopped and motioned with his hand.

I looked around. "Not much foot traffic," I said.

"It'll pick up as soon as the sun sets. The famous Soi Cowboy is down that road." He pointed. "You know what that is?"

"Let me guess. Go-go dancers?"

"You got it."

Chapter 19

Before the Creeper's arrival in Bangkok, Gai had heard about this man and his inability to stay the course and follow simple rules. He had a nasty habit of doing his own thing and ignoring the game. His time in Sydney, while successful, was also a disaster in terms of keeping the game under the radar. Instead of leaving after he had completed all the Attractions, the Creeper went on a rampage, slicing and dicing six other Australians. One of them was the man sent to remind him of his obligations to the game.

Gai took that last bit of information very seriously and had resorted to keeping a hidden blade on him. He had met the Creeper once, when the killer first arrived in Thailand, and wasn't looking forward to another encounter. It wasn't that Gai couldn't handle himself. He was more than able to take down another opponent. But there was something about the Creeper that, well, creeped him out.

Team Creeper had spent the first two weeks in Bangkok off the grid. Unless he engaged with the game, the team in charge of Bangkok's Chinatown Chase could not track his game play. Because of this, Gai had been sent to make contact and find out why there was a delay.

Participants were encouraged to make their way through the game as quickly as possible. It helped to ensure that they would not be caught, and it offset the chance of two teams playing the game in any one given city.

Gai remembered that day vividly.

He had received news that the Creeper had been holed up in a dingy hotel in the Silom area, near Patapong 3. The area was known more for its sex shows than its go-go dancers and was heavily visited by gay men because of the numerous gay-friendly bars and ladyboys who called the place home.

Gai never liked venturing into that part of town. Even during the day, the heavy stench from the previous nights revelry hung in the air and clung to clothing. But he forged ahead, ready to do the bidding of his boss, Somchai, no matter what the circumstances.

He slipped into the decrepit building and climbed three flights of stairs. He kept a fast pace, even when moving down the hall. When he knocked on the Creeper's door, a voice called out, "Come in."

Gai cautiously pushed the door open to reveal a dark room, save for the splinter of light that slipped through the sides of the drawn curtains. It took a minute for his eyes to adjust as he slid his hand up and down the wall, searching for the light switch.

"Don't," said the same voice. "The light hurts my eyes."

Gai stopped and focused his gaze toward the wall across from him where a shadowy figure sat in a chair. He closed the door and moved closer, hoping for more detail.

The figure rose out of the chair and took a step toward Gai. And another. Each was accompanied by the slow drag of a shoe across the floor. Step, drag. Step, drag. The figure closed in.

Gai held his ground. What could a lame man do to him? He had no reason to be afraid. Yet.

The figure drew closer. The scratchy sound of a leathered sole grating against the wooden floor grew louder. Gai could hear the man's heavy breathing but knew fatigue wasn't the cause. Was it excitement? With each step, the Creeper's breaths increased in speed, and Gai's eyes adjusted to the dark.

And then out of the blackness, the Creeper's face appeared into view a mere four inches away. Gai jerked back, caught off guard by the invasion of his personal space but not before a breathy mixture of garlic and sour violated his nose. Gai reached back toward the wall and located the light switch.

The man known as the Creeper flinched at the sudden invasion of artificial light.

"I'm not here to play games," Gai said calmly.

The Creeper lowered his arm from his eyes. "I don't get many visitors." He formed his words slowly before closing his mouth, leaving only a sliver of lip visible. Out of the corner of his light-gray eyes, deep, ravine-like wrinkles cut into his skin, creating a shadowing worthy of a horror makeup artist.

The Creeper raised his right hand and pointed at Gai. His nails were yellow, thick and sharpened into points. He reached out with his index finger, slowly moving toward Gai's cheek. "Your skin, it's so… inviting."

Gai moved his face away from the protruding finger and took a step back. "Why haven't you initiated the first Attraction in the game?"

The Creeper crinkled his brow, disappointed that the conversation had resorted to business. He much rather would have fingered Gai's cheek.

"If you must know, I'm not ready. I'm not in the mood for games at the moment."

Gai held the Creeper's gaze. It was important when dealing with people of this kind to never show weakness. He must appear to be an equal. "The rules state that you must engage the game within the first two days of arriving in a new city or risk disqualification."

"Disqualification!" the Creeper hissed. "You think you can threaten me?" The crinkle in his brow deepened, and his eyes narrowed. "*I* am in control of what I do, not you." He bared his teeth when he spoke.

Gai, stood strong. He realized the situation had turned grim. The wrong word or even a weak smile could worsen things. Gai kept his tone neutral and his wording even. "I am simply stating the rules that you agreed to abide by when you were accepted as a participant of the game."

"Accepted?" the Creeper's eyes widened. "Have you forgotten that, if not for people like me, this game would not exist? Without us, it is nothing."

Gai repeated the rule and left promptly after. He never forgot his initial conversation with the Creeper that day, and this time, he new what to expect during his second encounter.

The Creeper moved around a lot, preferring to change his location every three days. Since completing the first Attraction, he had relocated to a small hotel in the Phra Khanong neighborhood.

Gai felt for the seven-inch blade he kept in a leather sheath strapped to the waistband of his pants. He made no attempt to cover it, the bottom half protruding from his shirt. Up the stairs he went to the second floor and the last door at the end of the hall. After his quick knock, a voice called out for him to enter, just as it had with his last visit.

Gai expected the same intimidation tactics from the Creeper and had already mentally prepared himself. He wouldn't falter, not in the least. He turned the knob and pushed open the door. As expected, the curtains had been drawn shut and the lamps turned off. The bulb in the hallway was the only light source peering into the room.

"Close the door," the Creeper instructed from the darkness.

Gai waited a bit, wanting his eyes to adjust to the dark. Satisfied that he could make out shapes in the room, he closed the door. He ran his right hand along the wall, searching for a light switch. He wasn't about to have a conversation with the Creeper under those circumstances, again. A few seconds later, he felt what he was looking for.

The lone light on the ceiling flickered on, and Gai immediately sucked in a quick breath. The Creeper stood only inches away from him. Before he could react, even think, Gai felt an intense pain in his gut—a searing sensation that fanned out. He reached for his blade, but the pain increased tenfold. Any movement seemed to be met with more sharp pains.

What's happening? Try as he might, Gai could not glance down, not even for a second. His eyes remained transfixed upon the Creeper. He couldn't tear himself away. The Creeper held on to him with his narrow, beady eyes. They were dark. They were evil. They were the last thing Gai would ever see.

Chapter 20

The Creeper sat quietly on the uneven chair, humming a jazz song as he watched the dark fluid spill from the wound in Gai's midsection. He had used a carving knife to rip him open. He knew it would immobilize the man immediately. Sadly, this was a kill the Creeper received very little joy from. It was more of a necessity—a chore, really.

What the Creeper enjoyed most, what he longed for when toying with his victims, was a slow death. The longer his victims were kept alive while he played with them, the better. That's what satisfied his urges. It's what got him up in the morning.

The Creeper had become bored of the game and knew he would be in violation of the rules by abandoning his role as a participant; the rules were clear that everyone was expected to play until a winner was determined. Once they agreed, there was no turning back. No quitting. No taking a break.

But the Creeper didn't care about those silly rules. No one told him what to do. He had known the keepers of the game would send someone, and he had decided he would answer with a symbol as to what he thought of their stupid little diversion.

He stared at Gai a few moments before deciding it was time for him to move along and leave the body to do its job of conveying his message. He reached down and pulled up his right pant leg. Wrapped around his knee and running the length of his shin were two metal rods, one on each side. The homemade contraption made it difficult for the Creeper to walk. It made him limp.

He removed the device and stretched out his leg before standing. *Ah, much better.* He was a stickler for details. While he could have faked a limp, the device ensured that he limped consistently with every step.

He stood and walked perfectly toward the bathroom mirror, where he proceeded to remove the gray contact lenses he wore, revealing his light blue eyes. The Creeper blinked to clear his sight. He reached up and scratched near the corner of his left eye, which produced a flap of skin. He grabbed hold of it and removed the prosthetic, repeating the process for his other eye. Gone were the aged lines that gave life to his intense stare. He appeared younger, friendlier... trustworthy.

The Creeper reached up to the floppy mess of chestnut hair and pulled the rug off, uncovering his short but wavy blond hair. He put on wire frame glasses—fake—then changed into pressed khakis, a striped button-down, and brown loafers. Finally, he filed his nails down to a respectable length before using nail polish remover to rid them of that ugly, aging, yellow color.

He grabbed what few belongings he had and pocketed them before stepping around Gai and exiting the room.

Creep. Creep. Creep.

Chapter 21

Artie and I spent the rest of the afternoon planning our fake crime. We decided it would be best to set up for that night. The toilet was still Kang's best friend, but we had a job to do. I let him know what we were planning and that I would keep him updated.

With our location chosen, we headed over to a warehouse where the noodle carts were stored. The first thing I noticed when we got there was that the carts were attached to motorcycles. Instead of a sidecar, it had a side noodle cart.

"I hope you're not expecting me to drive that thing," I said.

Artie laughed. "Of course not. I'll drive."

Before I could question him more, I heard a woman shout Artie's name. He'd told me he had a close friend in the medical examiner's office, a specialist in bone reconstruction to help identify the dead. He said she could lend us a pair of realistic eyeballs. I spun around to see a stylish, chicly dressed woman walking toward us.

"That's the forensic scientist?" I whispered to Artie.

"Yes. She's different."

"What plans do you have for my expensive eyes?" she asked, her raised voice echoing slightly in the large space.

"Don't worry. Your eyes are safe with me. I'd like you to meet FBI Agent Abby Kane. She's investigating a case that is possibly tied to the human som tum we discovered a few days ago."

The woman finally made eye contact with me and stuck out her hand as she reached us. "Pleased to meet you. You can call me Tip."

"Nice to meet you, too," I said, smiling back at her.

"She's the best forensic investigator in the country," Artie added.

"Stop," she said, swatting at his arm playfully before focusing back on me. "So, FBI. Must be something important for you to come all the way out to Thailand."

I gave Artie a quick look. I wasn't about to discuss my business in Bangkok with just anybody, even if she was the country's best forensic investigator.

"It's fine, Abby. Tip is one of the good ones and is helping out on the som tum case."

I cleared my throat. "The FBI has reason to believe that the person behind the human som tum is part of a bigger organization. I'm hunting the person who runs it."

"And you think that person is here in Bangkok?"

"Possibly. I'll find out soon enough."

Tip grabbed hold of Artie's left hand and turned his palm up. "Here you go." She gently, almost teasingly, placed two realistic-looking eyeballs into it.

"They have serial numbers on the back," she continued, still holding his hand. "I expect the same ones to be returned." She flashed him a playful smile before letting go of his hand.

"You have my word, Tip."

Clearly the two had history, and I'm not talking as coworkers or friends. I kept my smile to myself.

Artie gave me an eye to look at. "What do you think?"

"Looks real. Might be a good idea to dress it up with some blood."

"Fish guts," he said. "Drip a little on each one, and it'll fool anyone into thinking they were just ripped out of someone's eye socket."

I didn't doubt it.

"I'm sorry I can't stick around," Tip said, "but I've got somewhere I need to be. Let me know if I can be of any more help."

With that, she left us as quickly as she had arrived. I turned to Artie. "She seems nice."

"Tip can be an asset. She just likes a lot of attention. That's all."

Yup, they definitely had history. For a brief second, I thought of fishing for more information about his relationship with her but decided against it. It wouldn't help the case, only my curiosity.

Once Tip had disappeared from view, it didn't take us

long to get the cart ready. We had everything we needed, even the noodles, which Artie claimed he could make. Transporting the cart to our location was the only concern I had.

"Wait, you were serious when you said you were driving this thing."

"Yes. Why not?"

"So should I find a taxi and meet you there?"

Artie gave me a strange look. "What are you talking about? We'll go on this."

That's when I put two and two together. "No way. I'm not riding on that death trap."

"Come on, Abby. It's safe. Everyone rides on motorbikes."

I wasn't arguing that. In the last few days, I'd seen men, women, sometimes even a family of four packed on to one bike as they weaved their way through traffic.

"You're lucky. You have jeans on—no need to sit sideways."

"I've seen those women sitting sidesaddle on the back of the motortaxis. I have no idea how they don't fall off."

Artie's mouth widened and his eyes disappeared into dark slits as he laughed. "It's called balance."

I watched him climb on board the rickety bike and give it a powerful jumpstart. The engine coughed to life before emitting a loud roar. A few throttle revs and he motioned for me to climb aboard. "You have nothing to worry about."

The only thought I could take solace in was that if we wrecked and I ended up in a hospital, I had on a pair of new underwear. I hopped on board, hung on tight and prayed we didn't end up playing bumper cars with a bus.

For the next twenty-five minutes, I got my fill of car exhaust while the wind whipped my hair into a crazy tangle. Artie eventually brought the bike to a complete stop near the curb, about fifty yards away from our location. He checked his watch. "Almost six-thirty. We will have missed most of the dinner rush, which is a good thing. I can control the scene for the setup. You should get off and wait for me here."

"Why?"

"It'll look suspicious if you're with me while I set up."

Artie explained that, even though I looked Asian, I wasn't Thai and I would still stand out. I didn't have a problem with that. I got off, and he continued on. While I waited, I put a call in to Kang.

"I'm really sorry about the situation," he said. "I wish I could be there helping."

"There's not much to do. This crime scene is very low-tech compared to what we orchestrated back in San Francisco. We'll wait an hour, and then Artie's men will arrive and conduct a quick investigation. The whole ordeal will probably take two hours, tops."

"Still, I feel bad."

"That's what you get for eating everything in sight," I

said, laughing.

"I know. And you warned me about that last vendor. Sheesh."

"What's the plan after you wrap up?"

"Not sure but I'll keep you posted."

"Okay. Great. Gotta go."

I hung up with Kang but not before hearing some questionable sounds coming from his end. I waited another fifteen to twenty minutes before Artie returned.

"Everything is in place, and I already snapped a few pictures" He showed me his phone. "Will this work?"

The eyeballs looked real. "Yes, this will do. Good call with the fish guts." I gave him my email address. "Send them to me."

Artie was spot on with the timing. From the moment we arrived until his men wrapped up their investigation and hauled away the noodle cart away, two hours had passed. He had impressed me, and I was starting to feel better about working the case with him. It was shortly after those thoughts that he turned to me with a smile and asked if I wanted to have dinner.

"I know a place where they serve great Isaan food."

"What's that?"

"Spicy."

Chapter 22

A maid at the small hotel discovered Gai's body later that same afternoon. It didn't take long for word of his demise to reach Somchai, thanks to a tip from a police officer who was friendly with Somchai's people. With the right amount of payoff, the body and the investigation had disappeared as quickly as the police were called to the hotel.

Somchai knew right away that the Creeper had gone off on his own again. That twisted farang had abandoned the game and was now running loose in his beloved Bangkok. Why did that matter? It endangered the game play, and it was Somchai's job to keep the game up and running. A participant wreaking havoc brought unnecessary attention, so the cover-up of Gai's body had needed to be quick and complete.

Somchai had no idea whether the Creeper would speak of the game, should the authorities catch him doing what he did best. Too much money and too many people were at risk, including Somchai himself. He would be the one to take the blame if he couldn't contain the situation. He had heard of what had happened to Jing Woo, the man charged with managing the game in San Francisco. It had been a convincing deterrent.

The first order Somchai gave to his men was to hunt down the Creeper. "You must find him before he commits another unauthorized kill."

Protocol required Somchai to report the altercation between Gai and the Creeper through the proper channels to the mastermind himself, whom he had never met. But Somchai believed it was better to present a problem with a solution in place rather than simply presenting the problem. If he could dispose of the Creeper first and then report the farang's inability to follow the rules of the game and his resulting elimination, that would keep Somchai's pride intact. And hopefully avoid a repeat of what had happened with Jing Woo.

From that point forward, Somchai repeatedly called his men every hour on the hour. The news remained the same: they were still searching for the Creeper.

It was midnight, and Somchai had grown restless with the situation. It shouldn't have taken long to track the man. He had a noticeable limp and moved slowly. *How hard can this be?* he thought while he paced the small office.

By his count, he had probably two days, perhaps three at the most, before the absent game play would trigger the application to send a message to him and those he reported to. Somchai couldn't prevent that from happening. The mastermind would be notified for a second time regarding Team Creeper's erratic game play.

However, Somchai was counting on his men to find the farang before that notice was generated. What he wasn't counting on was an unexpected call from the mastermind himself.

Chapter 23

I looked at my watch. It was a little after one in the morning. *Where had the time gone?* It had been almost five hours since we'd left our crime scene.

We'd started the night at a sidewalk restaurant on soi eighteen. There we dined on *tom yum hed*, a spicy sour mushroom soup, ate grilled pork neck, ravished som tum with raw crab, and devoured *tom yum talay*, a deliciously spicy mix of seafood and veggies. We had plenty of the local favorite, Leo beer, to wash it all down with.

I figured dinner had soaked up a solid hour and a half. We continued our drinking near my hotel at a bar that had outdoor seating with live music.

It turned out that Artie and I had a lot in common, both in terms of work and in terms of our outlook on life. He believed in the good, always striving to make his decisions and actions reflect that. So he said.

"I think that's why I love being a detective:" he went on, "It allows me the opportunity to help others."

Just then, our server placed a raised metal platter on our table. A large carp sat in an inch of bubbling soup thanks to a small can of chafing fuel below the pan. I watched Artie use his spoon and fork to deftly separate the white meat of the grilled fish from its tiny bones. I, on the other hand, needed my fingers and multiple stacks of napkins to get at the same meat. Even though we had eaten a full meal a few hours ago, like most Thais, Artie loved to eat, especially when drinking. My stomach didn't mind.

"How come you never married?" I switched to Jameson now that we had access to a fully stocked bar. The Irish whiskey loosened my mouth. I had no filter.

He shrugged. "I guess I haven't come across a woman who I've felt real love with. There were plenty I cared about, but I never felt that *real* love, love that allows you to accept the good, the bad, the rich, even the poor in others. You share those times together because you love that person."

Boy, did I know what he was talking about. I can honestly say I felt that way with Peng, my late husband. We were a team, living life together. And then life screwed me.

Artie threw the same question right back at me, and I found myself opening up about something I rarely discussed with others. But I felt like the conversation we had been having all night had been pretty revealing, so it was fitting. It was uplifting in a way. I didn't feel the need to keep up my guard. I could be real.

"I spent almost a year hunting the person who had murdered my husband but came up empty. I believe that's what caused me to burn out on the job."

"But you're still in law enforcement?"

"Yeah," I said, laughing. "Go figure."

"The job has a way of screwing us, yet we still love it."

I raised my glass. "That's the truth."

We both yawned simultaneously, a clear signal that the evening had come to an end. I had enjoyed a great time blowing off steam with Artie. I'm sure Kang would have enjoyed the night out too, but part of me was glad that he had remained at the hotel, resting on the toilet. It was selfish, but I liked having Artie to myself. Had Kang been here, the conversation would have been different. Not in a boring way, but different, less intimate.

Weirdly, Artie had momentarily filled a gap in my life that had been empty—the part that made me feel lonely, the part that only a *man* could fill. Yes, I had my family, and they brought me much happiness, but I missed having someone for me. Talking to Artie made those feelings of *want* disappear for a little while.

Artie offered to walk me back to my hotel. It was only a few sois away, not enough to merit a taxi. And I had all but sworn off riding on a motortaxi, especially with my balancing abilities in question.

"So you and Tip were an item," I said as we strolled along.

"Yes."

"I knew it the moment she walked into the warehouse."

"Really?" Artie stopped. "How?"

"I could tell by the way she looked at you. She still likes you."

"I know, but we're not right for each other. When we're together, it's either hot or it's cold. It's tiring, if you know what I mean."

"Yeah, great for make-up sex, but other than that..."

"A soap opera."

"So what's it like between you two now?"

"Our jobs keep us in contact, and occasionally we'll have lunch or dinner together, but sometimes..."

"Let me guess: you both have one too many beers and wake up the next morning in the same bed."

"It doesn't help. She's beautiful, fun, and not right for me," he said with a smile. "And the men in your life?"

"Rotten luck. I suck at choosing them."

Artie let out a burst of laughter, nearly losing his balance.

"I'm serious," I said adding my howls to his. "I can't catch a break."

"Maybe you're trying too hard."

I punched his arm playfully. "Or maybe not hard enough."

Artie threw his arm around me and pulled me in for a friendly hug while we walked. It was unexpected but felt nice. He wasn't the typical man I found myself attracted to, but I liked him. Sure he was interesting, and I felt comfortable around him but was I sexually attracted to him?

Not at the beginning of the night. But with my emotions heightened, his ability to temporarily cure my loneliness, and a whole bunch of alcohol running rampant through my system, I was open to the idea of whatever.

And not much later, that whatever came in the form of a kiss.

I'm not sure how we went from our playful conversation to a heavy make-out session outside the door of my hotel room, but it happened. I felt like a teenage girl coming back from a date except I didn't have to worry about my overprotective Irish father opening the door and pummeling my date for ravishing his daughter.

For every second our lip-lock continued, it pushed our working relationship into a dangerous territory. Artie was a great kisser, and I was slowly losing control of my ability to put a stop to what was happening. I knew if what we were doing moved to the other side of the door, we'd be waking up in the same bed the next morning. Not a good idea.

I had already made that mistake with a previous partner, and he'd ended up dead. Not because of me, but still...

I mustered up all the willpower I could and pulled away. And trust me when I say that, because it had been awhile since I'd had anyone fine-tune my engine.

Artie understood and didn't make a big deal about it. "You're right. We had a fun time, and things got a little out of control."

"Maybe more than a little."

He laughed at my joke. "Let's not let what happened tonight affect our work, okay?"

"I can do that," I said.

I gave him a hug goodbye and closed the door to my hotel room. A few minutes later I fell asleep midway through pleasuring myself. That's how Abby Kane rolls.

Chapter 24

Somchai had no idea why the mastermind had called him. He had never personally spoken to this person before. Any communication always came through a strict chain of command. Somchai initially thought Gai's death had been leaked and the mastermind had called for an answer. But that wasn't the case. The reason was for an entirely different matter: one involving the FBI agent and the SFPD detective.

"The two individuals pretending to be Team Carlson, have they solved the first Attraction?"

Somchai had been so concerned with fixing his Gai problem that he hadn't monitored the progress of Team Carlson. He quickly went to his laptop and saw that the team had uploaded a photo for approval.

"Yes, they have made an upload. I'm very sorry for my delay in forwarding the pictures on to you."

It was Somchai's responsibility to ensure that any submitted photos or video evidence met the game's guidelines. If that requirement were met, he would then forwarded the contents to the mastermind for approval. With that said, Somchai couldn't help but wonder how the mastermind had discovered that Team Carlson had made an upload. Somchai hadn't even known about it. He decided not to question but to only provide answers.

He promptly forwarded the pictures of the noodle cart containing the human eyeballs and waited on the phone. A few seconds passed before the voice on the other end spoke.

"The som tum from Team Creeper was better. How *are* Team Creeper's efforts coming along on the second Attraction?"

Is this a trick question? Does the mastermind know? Am I being tested? A flurry of thoughts raced through Somchai's head before he answered. "Team Creeper has been slow to start the second Attraction. Perhaps he wants to make another favorable impression."

"Good. That's helpful."

"If I might be so bold as to ask, how is that helpful?"

"I'm changing the second Attraction."

Somchai lowered the phone a bit as he took a moment to digest what he had just heard. "Will this change be for all teams playing through Bangkok?"

"No. It will only apply to Team Creeper. I'm excited to see what he delivers. He has become my favorite player. I will be waiting patiently. Ensure that there are no delays this time."

"Very well. I will familiarize my team with the new Attraction and make any necessary changes to the game play. We will not disappoint." Somchai waited for an answer but heard nothing, not even the slight wheeze he had heard earlier. The line had gone dead.

Somchai tapped away on his laptop, eager to see the new Attraction. What he saw made his stomach drop.

Chapter 25

I woke the next morning with a slight headache, nothing too terrible that a large glass of water and couple of aspirin couldn't tackle. After a quick shower, I changed into fresh clothing and put a call into Kang.

"Hi, Abby. I was just about to call you."

"How are you feeling?" I asked.

"Better. My stomach's no longer doing somersaults, and I don't think I need an adult diaper to leave my room."

"Too much information, but I'm glad you've regained control of your body."

Kang chuckled. I told him to meet me downstairs for breakfast, and I would bring him up to speed. I had already spoken to Artie that morning. The conversation wasn't awkward. He had a new witness for his human som tum case and wanted to track that person down. It was fine with me. I told him Kang and I would continue with the game play and that we could update each other when the time comes.

Twenty-five minutes later, Kang had a cup of coffee pressed to his lips, and I had my tea steeping in a mug. We both picked at a plate of fresh lychee and sliced dragon fruit.

"Everything went as planned last night, no hiccups." I showed Kang the pictures Artie had taken.

"That looks real," Kang said as he plucked a lychee from the plate and peeled off the reddish-pink rind.

"Fish guts. I uploaded a few photos after we finished rigging the crime scene and am now awaiting approval. Speaking of…" I reached into my bag and removed my laptop. I hadn't yet checked for an answer. "Let's see if we completed the task."

I fired up the game. A few seconds later, Kang and I were treated to a firework display congratulating us on our success. We gave each other a high five, and I then clicked on the second Attraction. We were hopeful that we might have caught up with the other team, since there had been no reports of another murder in the city yet.

We watched as the animated scroll unraveled, revealing our riddle.

Look up to find the cure for a Bangkok hangover.

"Look up to find the cure for a Bangkok hangover," Kang and I both repeated the phrase at once. I thought the hangover part of the riddle certainly made sense for a city known for indulging in libations, but the rest of the riddle made no immediate sense to me.

"What do you think?" I asked, looking at Kang.

He shrugged. "Definitely something having to do with partying."

"Yeah, I'm thinking the same thing. If we take the riddle literally, then it's about recovery. Maybe a food that helps with a hangover."

"A fruit from a tree?" Kang pushed his bottom lip up and shrugged.

"That's a thought. But if it's not literal, then the answer would only loosely tie into that theme."

We continued to stare at the laptop screen, thinking that would somehow reveal the answer.

"This can't be hard. We're the ones making it a chore," I said, stabbing my fork at a piece of dragon fruit. "Deranged psychopaths are figuring this stuff out. Why can't we?"

"Hey, give it a chance. We just got the riddle. Who knows how long it takes the others to figure this stuff out?"

"Not long, I'll tell you that. If it did, they wouldn't bother. They don't need the game to kill."

"Yeah, but you yourself said the gameplay can heighten the high they get from their kills, so…"

Sheesh, Kyle. Do you have to remember every single thing I say? I chewed and swallowed the sweet fruit before forking another piece. "Okay. Let's think this through like we always do. The riddles always tie into the city somehow through something iconic. What could tie Bangkok and hangover together that would make sense for a lot of people… Wait. *The Hangover* movie. The second one that takes place in Bangkok."

Kang snapped his fingers. "That's right. The riddle says to look up... The bar! The one with the gold dome on top of that tall building. It's where that Asian gangster, Chow, is arrested. That has to be the place."

Kang positioned the laptop in front of him and Googled the bar from the movie. A second later, results populated the browser page. "It's called the Sky Bar." He clicked on a picture of the rooftop bar, and it expanded in the browser.

"Looks like we're having drinks tonight," I said.

Chapter 26

The Creeper stood at the west entrance to Soi Cowboy as men of all ages and races shuffled by him, eager to experience the famous landmark and all its offerings. Above every bar were exuberant displays of neon signage that closely mimicked the Las Vegas strip: names like Sahara's, Rio, and Baccara were clearly homage to Sin City.

The Creeper had both hands resting comfortably inside the pockets of his black slacks. The top two buttons on his blue button-down shirt were undone, and his sleeves were rolled up to his elbows. It was business casual for the night. He was freshly shaved and wore cologne that would have most women turning their head to follow the scent.

After a few minutes of taking in the circus before him, the Creeper walked confidently down the soi. *Creep. Creep. Creep.*

Young women, scantily clad in their uniforms resembling either sexy cheerleader outfits or the wardrobe from a Victoria's Secret runway show, stood outside their respective bars, enticing men to come inside. It didn't take long for them to notice the handsome farang with the sexy bed hair.

"Hey, good-looking, come with me," squealed a tiny woman wearing a sequined halter top with matching short shorts. She latched both hands onto his right arm and pulled him, with surprising force, toward her bar.

The Creeper smiled. *If you only knew. If you only knew.*

He shook his arm loose only to have two other women from the bar opposite clamp onto him and try their luck. The Creeper indulged them and playfully resisted all the way to the bar's outdoor seating. He again shook his arm free, smiled and walked away.

The Creeper wasn't eager to settle for the first piece of arm candy that came his way. He knew there were over twenty bars to peruse and hundreds of girls to choose from. Plus, he had an advantage.

Not only was the Creeper a white farang, considered the most handsome of foreigners by Thai women, but he was also a seriously good-looking one. His looks were good enough that a working girl might even throw him a freebie, something almost all visiting men were largely unsuccessful at obtaining.

He continued his slow walk, ignoring the calls of the women and, instead, allowed the thumping dance music from each bar to fill his ears. His head swayed from side to side as he marched down the aisle, shopping.

The Creeper was in search of something special—innocence—a girl fresh from the rural countryside of Thailand, one that had not become jaded or turned into a calculating businesswoman. He wanted a girl who would genuinely like him, one who over time would even be convinced that he was there to whisk her away from this life—her prince in shining armor. It would make the kill so much more pleasurable.

At the end of the soi, the Creeper stopped and faced one of the most popular bars on the strip: Baccara. He knew he would end up there, but still he shopped the other venues on the way, giving them an opportunity to win his business.

Satisfied he had seen nothing of worth yet, he stepped up onto the wooden platform that led the way to a curtained door manned by a bouncer. Inside the bar, urban hip-hop thumped against his chest, and his eyes settled on the stage in front of him. Standing on a lighted floor were no fewer than twenty bikini-clad women in stilettos, gyrating for the audience of men who occupied stadium seating around the bar.

The Creeper did a onceover and saw that there were no available seats; there wasn't even standing room in the aisle. He looked up above the stage to the ceiling, which was actually the bottom of the see-through stage on the second floor. From below, everyone had a clear view of the dancers in their mini-skirts. None of them wore any underwear. *The girls upstairs are better anyway*, he thought as he maneuvered his way through the crowded aisle.

At the top of the stairs, he faced an equally packed sitting area, but a nearby mama-san noticed his predicament and approached him. "How many?"

He held up one finger and smiled.

She returned the smile before grabbing his arm and leading him to a corner table for two near the stage that had just been vacated.

"What you want?" she asked as she mimicked taking a sip from a bottle in her hand.

"Singha," he replied.

After she left his table, the Creeper turned his attention toward the ladies swaying their hips in front of him. It didn't take long for the dancers to notice him and begin posturing for his attention. They smiled. They winked. They shimmied their breasts. A few went so far as to bend over and wiggle their behinds, ensuring he had a good look at the goods on offer.

They all wanted to spend time with him. What was there not to like? Sex with a handsome man was better than sex with a fat, unattractive one, no matter how rich he appeared to be. And the Creeper knew this.

One song later, a shift change occurred allowing the girls to exit the stage. One by one, they made their way to the Creeper; some even ignored the calls of other men to sit with them. The smiling prize at the corner table was too much of a draw. They knew one of them would go back to his hotel; why not be the lucky one?

Chapter 27

The smell made him gag.

Artie brought his arm up over his nose to help mask the rotten stench, but it did little to help. Another officer walked over to him and offered him a small bottle of aroma oil. Artie thanked him and put a dab under his nose. It barely worked, but it would have to do.

The naked body of a young woman still lay tied to the bed, marinating in its own bodily fluids, though most of it had soaked into the thin mattress. The femur bone was visible in both thighs, as if an animal had gnawed on each leg right down to the bone. But Artie knew that wasn't the case. Off to the side of the bed lay the culprit—a metal grater. Bits of dried flesh still lay trapped in its teeth.

The walls of the studio apartment had been covered in gray egg crate foam, and the window had been nailed shut. The poor girl could have screamed her heart out, and the neighbors wouldn't have heard a peep.

Her purse sat on a table with her belongings still inside: a wallet, a cell phone, makeup, a toothbrush, deodorant, facial cleanser, and a few other toiletries—a mini-travel bag typical for a bar girl. It contained everything they needed to clean up after seeing a customer, especially if they spent the night.

Artie noticed a few crumpled bar receipts from the Shark bar. He tried the phone, but it was locked, though a selfie of the girl served as the wallpaper. Artie had seen enough. He let his men know he had both the girl's phone and identification before leaving the apartment.

He hopped onto his motorbike and zoomed between cars and buses until he arrived at Soi Cowboy. Thong Lo police officers were always stationed at the eastern entrance to the soi. He knew most of them. It was their job to keep order in the area, and they did so with an iron fist.

Artie nodded at the men before heading straight for the Shark bar. It was the second one on the right and one of the most popular on the tiny strip. Pretty girls in white skin-tight dresses stood outside. Their job was "reception". They did their best to corral men inside and also to provide company to those who sat outside to drink and people-watch. He knew one of them, a young brunette named Pla. She couldn't have been older than twenty-two.

She smiled pleasantly at Artie as he approached. "Hi, Artie. Come to see me tonight?"

"Sorry. I'm on duty."

She lowered her face and let her bottom lip quiver. "You never come to see me," she said softly. She then hooked her arm around his and quickly produced a fresh smile. "I'll take you to see mama-san."

Pla knew that Artie was a detective and that there was only one reason he would ever come inside the bar. She led him past a crowd of Japanese men who stood frozen just inside the entrance. Their mouths gaped as they stared at the line-up of young girls dressed in barely-there clothing.

Pla maneuvered Artie around the gawkers and up four flights of narrow stairs to where the head mama-san had her office. Pla gave Artie a friendly squeeze to the arm and a peck on the cheek before leaving.

A woman in her mid-fifties looked up from her seat behind a desk. Her long black hair hung past her shoulders. Streaks of gray were starting to make their appearance, but the chestnut-brown skin on her face remained smooth and relatively free of wrinkles. Her eyebrows narrowed, and her quiet demeanor disappeared as she realized who stood before her.

"Artie," she called out. She slapped an open palm against the desk. "Why are you harassing me? What did I do?"

Artie shook his head, not sure why he deserved this attitude. He had known the mama-san, Jay, for over fifteen years.

She waved a dismissive hand at him and further crinkled her brow. "Don't act like you don't know what I'm talking about. Your men came into my bar tonight and shut me down for one hour. What bullshit is this? Huh? What did I do?"

It all made sense to him now. Every so often, the officers stationed at the eastern entrance to Soi Cowboy would enter a club to make sure all business licenses were up to date, all girls working were of legal age, and to inspect whatever else they felt like checking.

During this time, business in the bar literally came to a halt. The lights were turned on. The music was shut off. The girls stopped dancing, and no alcohol was served. The customers inside usually sat there perplexed as the girls tried to keep them calm and prevent them from fleeing. These impromptu visits cost the bar and the girls a lot of money.

"Sorry, Jay. You know I don't control what they do."

"Bullshit!"

The conversation was fast becoming a losing battle and a waste of Artie's time. He pulled out the cell phone he had taken from the crime scene earlier and showed the picture of the girl to the mama-san.

Jay stood and leaned across the desk for a closer look. "Where is she?" she asked, placing her hands on her hips. "It's been over one week since she's been to work. She never told me she wanted to holiday." Jay's aggravation levels continued to rise. She was now pacing the small office, waving her arms around to emphasize her words. "You know I don't have time for this girl. You tell her I cut, cut, cut. One thousand baht every day."

"Jay." Artie tried to get a word in. "Jay…"

"If she doesn't come back, I cut salary. I cut everything."

Jay continued with her rant, prompting Artie to finally grab the woman by both arms and give her a little shake. "Jay, calm down. This girl, she works here?"

"Yes, Kim works here. Six months, now. Where is she?"

"We found her body tonight. She's dead."

Jay sucked in a quick breath before her legs gave way. Artie moved quickly to catch the stunned woman before she crumpled to the floor. He gently sat her down and watched the tears build in her eyes before spilling over. She had gone from raving lunatic to distraught mother in a mere heartbeat.

"No, no, no," she said softly. "Not Kim. She was a good girl. I love all my girls, but Kim—she was special."

Artie didn't doubt that Jay loved her. The fines that she imposed on her girls for not coming to work or being late were strictly business and didn't affect how she felt about them. She had been a second mother to most.

"I think a customer was responsible."

Jay wiped at her tears with the back of her hand before looking at Artie. "Customer? Why?"

Artie described what the man might have looked like. "Think, Jay; do you remember or maybe your staff can—"

"I don't remember seeing this man." Energy returned to her movements as she stood.

"What about the other mama-sans? Think they might

know more?"

"Maybe. I don't know. I told you: Kim hasn't shown up for work in over one week."

Artie decided to breach the subject of Kim trying out a new venue for work. It could be a touchy subject, but he had a case to solve. "Jay, do you think it's possible Kim was working at another bar?"

"Work someplace else?" Jay's eyes shot up toward Artie. "I don't know; maybe that's why she hasn't come to work. She makes good money here. I don't know why she would want to go work at another bar."

Artie had found one other lone receipt in Kim's bag. It was for a bar at Nana Plaza. His next stop.

Chapter 28

The Carlsons, a.k.a. Kyle and I, had cleaned up and were ready to party. We set off at around nine that night for our excursion to the Lebua Hotel, which housed the famous rooftop Sky Bar. We had opted to dress casually, as most tourists do, rather than to wear appropriate cocktail attire with our disguises. I knew we were heading out for one reason, but I had already decided to play up the tourist role by snapping a bunch of pictures for Ryan and Lucy and, of course, grabbing a cocktail for myself from one of the world's highest open-air bars.

It was a straight shot up to the sixty-fourth floor rooftop. The doors opened and we were immediately greeted by restaurant staff and guided to the bar. A few steps later, we exited the gold-topped dome and faced the most amazing cityscape view I had ever seen. It shut me up for a good minute.

I stood and stared until Kang nudged me forward, down a flight of stairs to where the actual bar was situated. I continued walking right up to the edge of the granite-tiled terrace, where three to four feet of neatly manicured bushes kept people safely away from the short stucco wall that wrapped around the rooftop. There I drew a long breath and settled into a content smile.

From up here, the city shook off its red-light glow and sparkled like the kings' jewels. The Chao Phraya could be seen snaking its way around magnificent skyscrapers that punched upwards into the night like electronic candlesticks. Surely no photograph could fully capture and translate what on-site gazing could deliver.

We spent a solid half hour fixated on the view, which allowed me to take thirty-plus pictures with my phone. Only ten were selfies. I posted a few of the pictures to my Instagram account and texted Ryan and Lucy about the upload. It didn't take long for the kids to respond with a barrage of text messages.

Eventually, Kang and I pulled ourselves away and went to work, posing as Team Carlson. This time, we knew to look for the young girl from the temple, the one who had given us the answer to our last riddle. We headed straight to the bar and got drinks, and then strolled along the rooftop, keeping our eyes peeled for our target. She could be dressed as an employee of the restaurant or even a guest, like ourselves. I didn't mind the slow walk while I sipped my Jameson.

Kang spotted her first. "There she is. One o'clock, selling roses."

We positioned ourselves in her path and a few minutes later, she approached Kang and asked if he would like to buy me a rose. "Only 700b," she told him. Kang started to balk at the price. I playfully hugged him. "Aww, come on sweetie; that's like twenty-three bucks." I also threw my elbow into his side to remind him of why we were here.

Kang pulled out his wallet and handed the girl a 1,000b note while mentioning the name of the game. In return, she handed me a rose with gold wrapping along the stem—the only one in her basket to have it. Kang held his hand out and waited for his change. The girl smiled at him before turning away. I threw another elbow into his side before he could protest.

We walked to an area where the foot traffic was minimal before I said anything. "I wonder if 'rose' is our answer."

Kang shrugged. "Could be. If not, we'll just run down the list: red rose, gold wrapping, 700b…"

I went ahead and removed the gold wrapping around the stem. Written on the inside was the phrase *The Big Mango*.

"Mango?" Kang had pulled his chin back, giving himself a pair of them.

"Yeah, it's a nickname for Bangkok. I take it you've never heard of it."

Kang drained the last of his beer before looking at his watch. "It's a little after ten. Should we head back to the hotel and punch in the answer?"

I was about to nod my head in agreement but hesitated.

"You know what? Let's have one more drink, then we'll head back. We're not robots. We need a little R&R from time to time."

"Good move, Agent." Kang wasted no time heading back to the bar to grab us another round, and I went back to enjoying the rooftop sights.

By the time we planted our feet back on street level, it was 11:00 p.m. Still, there was no shortage of sightseers funneling themselves into the building for a drink at the famous bar. We pushed through the crowd and onto the sidewalk that was lined by six or seven food vendors.

We both stopped in front of a cart that sold grilled pork. It was as if our stomachs had read each other's minds. The vendor moved his hand along the small grill, flipping the skewered morsels of tender meat over one by one. The red-hot coals seared from the fatty drippings, sending billowing gray straight up my nose. It smelled like my kind of heaven. Kang motioned for two. I quickly told him I wanted two for myself. He smiled and then changed the two fingers he held out to four.

We stood by the vendor while we munched until a taxi tout approached us. "Taxi? I have taxi, take you hotel."

We needed a taxi, so we followed the man. He led us down the soi, away from the vendors and toward a dark alley. Kang and I stopped. It was obvious to us there was no taxi there. Before we could turn and head back to where the vendors were situated, four men appeared from the darkened alley and closed in.

The one nearest us wrapped his arms around me, immobilizing my arms. I instinctively threw my head back into his face. He cried out and released me. I followed up with a hard elbow to his gut. From the corner of my eye, I could see Kang engaged in his own fight with two men. I wasn't worried about him; I had already seen what the guy could do.

I wasn't in the mood for a street fight and had my weapon tucked away in my purse. I quickly backed away from my attacker to buy me time to get to it, but another man had already closed in, and he kicked my purse right out of my hands. Perhaps he sensed what I was about to do, or perhaps he just got lucky with his kick. Either way I was faced with what my father lovingly called "a swingin' donnybrook".

I raised both arms into a defensive position and easily blocked two fist strikes from the man who had kicked my purse away. I wasn't so lucky with the leg kick into my side. I doubled over from the pain and took an elbow to the face. It was then that I realized he was a skilled fighter—Muay Thai, possibly. Before I could recover fully, he struck a third time and in seconds had me kissing the street.

Kang held his ground against his two attackers. He,

too, quickly realized both were trained in Muay Thai, but their level of skill wasn't enough to overcome the detective's lifelong pursuit of mastering the art of kung fu.

It didn't take long for Kang to deliver two perfect tiger strikes to one of his attackers. He heard the dull snap of a rib and watched the man double over. He clamped his hands on the back of the man's head and followed up with a knee strike to his face. The man was unconscious before he hit the asphalt.

That's when something hard hit the back of Kang's head, sending him down to one knee. Dazed and with his sight blurred, he never saw the foot rushing straight toward his face, snapping his head back.

Kang's instincts took over, and he covered up with his arms as he anticipated another blow, fearful of what would happen should he take another direct hit. Another kick did come, but his arms soaked up the bulk of the impact. By then, his eyesight had righted, and he fended off yet another strike from the man's leg.

Kang retaliated with a foot sweep, knocking his attacker to the ground. He pounced onto the man's chest and delivered a fury of fist strikes until his attacker lay unconscious.

Kang rose to his feet quickly, arms up, ready to defend or strike. He knew at least four men had attacked them. Spinning around, his balance still a bit wobbly, he counted three men on the street. The two near him were not moving.

A wooden bat lay next to one of them. The third man lay a few feet away, moaning. The fourth was nowhere to be seen. He had disappeared. And so had Kane.

Chapter 29

Kang reached inside his coat and felt his weapon sitting securely in its holster. A relief, considering a crowd of Thais had gathered around him; they didn't look friendly.

He removed his wallet from his back pocket and held up his badge. "I'm a police officer," he said, not sure if anyone understood him. They didn't.

The crowd's concern wasn't that Kang had just been attacked or that he had in his possession a badge, but that he had just attacked one of their own. And it wasn't pleasing to them.

"They attacked me first," he continued. "You saw that, right?"

Kang's pleas went unheeded. Members of the crowd, made up of food hawkers and motortaxi drivers, shouted at him while pointing at their fallen compatriots. Kang didn't know what they were saying, but he didn't like their tone.

At this point, the crowd of angry Thais formed a circle around him. He had to remove himself from the situation. Fast. He looked around for an escape route but saw something better.

He approached a motortaxi. "Sorry, pal." Kang pushed

the owner off the bike and hopped on. He hit the electronic starter and gunned the engine before the confused man could react. Off he went, weaving the bike around the mob. In the process, he took a few blows but eventually bypassed them all. But Kang wasn't out of the woods yet.

He looked back to see that the other motortaxis had given chase. There were six closing in on him. Kang twisted the throttle back and sped down the soi. He had no idea where he was headed—he hoped not deeper into the neighborhood.

The only thought Kang had managed at that moment had been to make it to the safe house that he and Kane had secured at another hotel. It had been Kane's idea to book an extra room at a different hotel as a just-in-case. If something did go wrong, they both knew to head to that location.

Up ahead, a sea of red brake lights lit up the dark street. Kang did what he saw every other person in Bangkok do while riding a motorbike: He threaded the traffic and drove between the cars.

A large truck shrunk the gap up ahead, and Kang didn't like the odds of trying to squeeze by. He slowed and drove between the front and back of two cars, heading for the other Thai road: the sidewalk.

Not a smart move.

It was crowded with vendors and their customers. The horn on the bike bleated out as Kang shouted for the shopping crowd to clear the path, but not before he knocked a few to the ground. That slowed him down enough for one of his pursuers to ride up alongside of him and start punching him. Kang used his long leg to kick the front wheel of the other motortaxi, causing the man to lose control and crash into a vendor's table full of fake Rolex watches.

Shouts and screams erupted behind Kang as he sped off. He had extinguished one of his pursuers, but another quickly filled the spot right behind him. The rest were still giving chase from the road. Kang knew he had to get off the sidewalk. It slowed him down.

To make matters worse, the sidewalk made a sharp left up ahead. He would have to slow his bike considerably to make the turn. He had maybe thirty seconds to figure out a plan. As he closed in, he realized the sidewalk actually turned into steps that led to a bridge. Not an ideal situation. But there was another option. One that Kang wasn't thrilled about.

He gunned the engine of the motorbike, and it picked up speed. He watched the speedometer climb: 60km, 80km, 100km. He feared the old bike would never reach its top speed of 160km. He could already hear the engine straining while the vibration in the handlebars became increasingly worse.

Kang aimed the bike toward a narrow wooden table that had been leaned against a low wall—a makeshift ramp. He was about to attempt a jump of epic portions, one that

Ty Hutchinson   135

the famous daredevil Evel Knievel would never have undertaken.

Kang had no idea what the span of the canal was or whether he had enough speed to propel himself safely to the other side. Or even if there was another side. He hoped there was one. He took one last look at the gang of motorbikes chasing him before gripping the handlebars tighter. He lowered his head and prayed he wasn't making the stupidest decision ever.

Within seconds, the motorbike hit the ramp and launched into the air. Kang let out a yell as the bike sailed off in the darkness over what he could only imagine was a watery staph infection waiting to envelop him. His eyes searched for the other side, but all he saw was blackness. Doubt, then regret, filled his mind. *What the hell did I just do?*

The engine of the 135cc bike whined as Kang held the throttle open, hoping that somehow it would add to the propulsion of the bike. But as fast as the bike rose, it started to fall. Gravity had sunk its hooks into the flying machine and was beginning to pull it back to Earth.

Kang's high-pitched scream echoed into the night as he readied himself for an unavoidable crash landing into a polluted canal. But no sooner had that thought crossed his mind than hope appeared in the form of a flat, cement embankment, one that led to a road.

Kang knew he could stick that landing. He was sure of

it. A perfect touchdown would set him free from his pursuers. He just needed to reach the other side. But there was one problem. The bike was falling short.

Chapter 30

A dark bag sporting a smell reminiscent of motor oil had been secured over my head, eliminating my ability to see or even detect the slightest source of light, but still, I knew I had been thrown into the trunk of a vehicle. The sound of an engine, jerky movements, and a bad suspension that sent periodic jolts into my spine only confirmed the obvious.

I didn't squander any precious time trying to decipher how I had ended up in that situation. That was an answer I could ponder later, after I escaped, which was my only concern at the time. Instead, I kept track of how many turns and stops the vehicle made. I wasn't sure if it would help, but I did it anyway like my life depended on it. It probably did.

For twenty minutes, I made mental notes of the vehicle's movements. There were many things to count, and I worried I would start to lose track. But no sooner had that thought waltzed into my mind than the vehicle came to a stop, and the engine shut off.

I could hear the voices of two Thai men speaking and the crunch of gravel from their footsteps nearing. A beat later, I heard the click of a latch. Rough hands grabbed me by my arms and yanked me out of the trunk. My legs flailed for a second before finding their footing on the ground.

I could still only detect the two men, but I had to assume there might be more. They each grabbed an arm and ushered me forward, grunting in Thai. Left and right they jerked me forward. I wondered for a second if they were drunk but tossed that thought. I was pretty sure one of my captors was part of the group of men that had ambushed Kang and me.

The two men dragged me forward until my feet bumped up against stairs. Up we went, me half walking, half being carried. I counted five flights of stairs. We walked for what felt like another ten feet before we stopped abruptly. I heard a knock on a door, then I felt a whoosh of cool air before my captors escorted me into an air-conditioned room.

After a few steps, one of them forced me to sit down on a metal chair. A hand grabbed the bag that covered my head but not before more discussion took place. I could only guess that my captors were debating whether they should remove it.

Seconds later, I sucked in a deep breath as the manufactured air chilled my hot and sweaty face. I struggled to open my eyes, but the light in the room stung, forcing me to squint at best. I could see that there was a desk in front of me with someone sitting behind it. I decided against speaking and focused on regaining my eyesight.

"Do you know why you are here?" The male voice had a Thai accent and came from across the desk. I shook my head no.

"We're here to help you, Agent Kane."

They know who I am?

"There is a man killing women in Bangkok. We can give you information that will help you capture him."

Who is killing women? Is this about the game? A million thoughts raced through my mind as I worked to comprehend what he had said to me. "Who are you, and how do you know who I am?"

"Agent Kane, we've known about you for some time."

This has got to be about the game. "Are you the mastermind behind the Chinatown Chase?"

"The man you're after calls himself the Creeper."

I know that name from the leaderboard. Team Creeper is in Bangkok. "I'm supposed to know who that is?"

"Don't pretend to be stupid, Agent. You know what this is about."

By now, my eyesight had normalized and allowed me to look directly at the plump man behind the voice, except he wore a clear plastic mask that disguised his face. It was disturbing.

He went on to give an accurate description of what we knew the Creeper to look like, but still, I didn't know why the people behind the game were helping me to catch one of

their players. Perhaps they had lost control of him and
wanted him eliminated, literally. Or they were setting me
up.

"How do I know you're not lying to me? Surely you
must know how odd this conversation is," I asked.

"He made som tum out of human flesh."

Okay, he got that right. "Why are you helping me?
Answer that."

"Catch him, Agent Kane, and we'll answer all your
questions."

"You seem to think that the information you've given
me is revolutionary. It's nothing we didn't already know.
You've got to give me more."

"If you wish. The Creeper has completed the first
Attraction and will soon take on the second one."

"So he'll head over to the Sky Bar like I did tonight for
an answer to the riddle?" I was unsure about Kang's status,
so I decided not to acknowledge him.

"No."

My patience with his cryptic answers started to run
thin. I let out a breath. "Are you telling me the game play
differs for each player?"

"The Creeper has a specific task for completing the
second Attraction, one that will lead him right to you."

"Really? I'm all ears."

"He's been ordered to eliminate Team Carlson."

Chapter 31

The back wheel of the motorbike took the brunt of the impact as it fell short of the embankment. The jolt that followed sent Kang up and over the handlebars, flying through the air like a wannabe superhero, but Kang had the mindset to tuck into a roll as he landed, minimizing what surely would have been an impressive amount of road rash.

Kang lay on his back, dazed for a brief moment, before hurrying to his feet. He scanned the bridge and saw the motorbike gang fighting their way through the crowd. Kang turned and ran in the opposite direction toward a taxi that had just dropped off a fare. He jumped in the back seat.

"The Sheraton on Sukhumvit," he called out in an even tone, not wanting to alert the driver. His torn and soiled suit had already caused the young man to give pause on whether he should take the fare. Not wanting to take any chances, Kang offered up a flat rate as opposed to using the meter. "Three hundred baht," he said, knowing the fare would only have been about 90 baht if the meter had been used. The driver jiggled the stick shift into gear and took off. Money talks.

The yellow and green cab sped down Rama IV Road

heading southeast before turning onto Asoke Road and continuing north. From there, it was a straight shot to Sukhumvit. Kang patted his back pocket and felt his wallet, but his cell phone was gone. All he could surmise was that he must have lost it in the crash. At least he still had his weapon.

The Sheraton was near the Asoke skytrain stop. Unfortunately before reaching it, the cab slammed into stop-and-go traffic. Mostly stop. At the rate the cab continued to inch along the road, Kang figured he could make better time on foot and exited the vehicle. It didn't take long for him to notice the stares. He took another look at his tattered suit and realized it wasn't helping him to blend in.

Custom tailor shops hawking "suits in a day" littered the Sukhumvit area. Kang figured a fresh change of clothes would go a long way considering he had no idea if he was still being followed. He walked twenty feet before spotting Raji's Fashions. A sign on a sandwich card outside the shop touted 399b suits. The price was right, and Kang made a left turn into the store.

Inside, a short, Indian man with a round belly greeted Kang and quickly gave him a cautious once over before grinning. "Hello, my friend. Rough night?"

"You can say that."

"Okay. You've come to the right place. We tailor the best suits in all of Bangkok."

"Can you give me something now?" Kang watched the

smile on the salesperson's face disappear.

"My friend, it is late. I can deliver a new suit tomorrow evening."

"Not good enough. I need something now. There must be something you can do. I don't want to take my business elsewhere." Kang looked outside the shop as if he were already considering that thought.

The salesperson took a second to realize Kang's seriousness before whipping out a tape measure. Twenty minutes later, Kang exited the shop wearing one of the outfits from a mannequin. The pants were a bit short, but the rest of the beige ensemble fit his frame relatively okay.

Feeling better about his appearance, Kang continued north until he reached Sukhumvit Road. Thais and tourists trafficked the area thanks to the numerous bars and restaurants, the Terminal 21 shopping center and the Soi Cowboy entertainment center.

Along the way, he passed a street vendor selling disposable phones and purchased one. Kang topped up the SIM card at a nearby 7/11 before dialing Kane's cell but got voicemail. He left a message that he was heading out for a bite to eat—code for heading to the safe location. Kang had another number to call. He dug through his wallet and pulled out the business card Artie had given him.

"Artie, it's Kyle."

"Detective, I'm glad you called. We got a break in the som tum case. I was—"

"Artie, we got ambushed tonight."

"What?"

"A bunch of thugs jumped us as we were leaving the Lebua hotel. We had gone there to visit the Sky Bar and collect our answer to the second riddle."

"Wait, are you sure this wasn't a mugging?"

"Positive. We were led to a group of men by a taxi tout."

"But who—"

"It has to be someone connected with the game. No one else in Thailand, except for your department, knows we're here and why."

Artie blurted out a barrage of questions, seeking more information, but Kang stopped him. "Artie, listen to me. I'm okay, but Abby...she's missing. I need your help."

Kang explained that he couldn't return to the Landmark Plaza because someone could be waiting there for him. He also didn't want to let Artie know that he and Abby had a safe location. At that moment, Kang didn't trust anyone. He would only give the Thai detective the information needed to help find Abby. Artie told Kang to meet him on the first floor of the Terminal 21 shopping center in twenty minutes.

Kang figured he was ten minutes away by foot and moved quickly to get there before Artie. Not wanting to take any chances, he ducked inside a men's clothing store and waited. The detective was true to his word and showed up at the mall right on the twenty-minute mark. Kang approached him from behind

"Artie," he said placing a hand on the detective's shoulder.

Artie jumped. "Are you okay?" he asked, looking Kang over after regaining his composure.

"I'm fine. Is there a place here where we can talk privately?" Kang asked, looking around.

"Yes. Upstairs on the fifth floor, there's a quiet bar."

Artie led the way up a multitude of escalators. Neither of them said anything until they were tucked away in a corner table that overlooked the surrounding hotels.

Once the server left with their drink order, Kang told Artie everything that had happened to him from the moment he and Kane had left the Sky Bar until he had contacted the Thai detective.

"And you never saw the men take her?"

"No. At least, that's what I think happened. It had to have."

"You have a phone now. Did you try calling her?"

"Yes, but all I got was voicemail." Kang tried Abby's cell once more. A few seconds later, he shook his head. "I'm getting voicemail. There's a chance she might not have her phone."

Artie watched Kang put the cell down on the table. "Just so you know, I already have men heading over to the hotel to question the vendors and taxi drivers. If we act now, there's a good chance we can get information that might lead to finding her."

Kang's eyes met the detectives. "Don't take this the wrong way, but how confident are you that it'll help?" Kang didn't want to come off as distrusting of the efforts of the Thai police, but he had to ask.

"Sometimes we find people; sometimes we don't. Let's hope we're lucky this time around."

Chapter 32

Kang felt a little better after talking to Artie. "I'll go back to the Lebua hotel with you. The vendors may know something about the men who attacked Abby and me."

"Look, that's not a good idea. I know she's your partner and you want to help, but trust me on this one. It'll only cause more problems."

"What do you mean? I can finger the vendors who were there. Some of them even attacked me as I tried to escape."

"This is Thailand, not America. It's better if a Thai person deals with these people."

"I understand," Kang conceded somewhat begrudgingly.

After the two made their way back outside, Kang waited until Artie took off on his motorbike before making his way to the Sheraton Hotel. It wasn't far from the shopping center, across the busy Sukhumvit Road and another fifty or so yards west.

He and Kane had already collected two key cards for the room and hid them independently in separate locations. Kang had no idea where Kane had put hers and vice versa.

Most of the sidewalks in Bangkok were made of square bricks. Kang had found a loose tile near a bush, and that's where he hid his card and hoped it had remained.

When he reached the location, he sat down on a foot-high perimeter wall that separated the hotel property with the sidewalk. When no one was passing by, he lifted the loose stone. Underneath, he spotted the white hotel card and quickly pocketed it.

A few minutes later, Kang exited the elevator on the twentieth floor of the hotel and headed to room 2077. He drew his weapon before pressing his ear up against the door, listening for a few seconds. Hearing nothing, he inserted the card key into the slot above the doorknob and entered the room. It was empty, and he saw no signs that Kane had been there. He had hoped that she had.

Kang used the hotel phone to call his partner's cell once more but, again, got her voicemail. *Where are you, Abby?*

There was nothing more for Kang to do there. He left a message on the hotel's pad of paper that he had gone out for a smoke—code for their original location.

Kang thought it was important to head back to the Landmark and retrieve the laptop. There wasn't much more he could do at the moment in the search for Abby aside from calling her contact at the embassy and alerting the cavalry, but that would only hurt their chances at capturing the mastermind.

A big part of their advantage was their ability to keep their game play under the radar. Kang guessed their cover was already blown—it had to have been—but still, bringing more attention to the game by having a team of FBI agents fly into town to help find one of their own only drew more attention. *Abby's a capable agent and can handle herself,* he reminded himself. He had to trust that she was okay.

Kang exited the hotel and headed west on Sukhumvit to the Landmark Plaza. It was a fifteen-minute walk away. It was nearing one-thirty in the morning, but the sidewalks were still busy, mostly with packs of men.

Kang knew Bangkok's red-light districts were lively, but what surprised him was that it wasn't contained to those two areas. The entire stretch of Sukhumvit Road from Soi Cowboy to Nana Plaza was one big party. Women, booze, and a variety of restaurants were readily available, in that order. A lonely man did not exist in Bangkok.

Kang continued his quick walk and politely declined the repeated requests for a drink by the women who sat at the sidewalk bars. When he reached the hotel, he waited outside until he saw a large contingent of Japanese businessmen entering. He slipped within their ranks and walked with them through the lobby and into the elevator.

Kang exited on the fifteenth floor of the Landmark and walked a short way to room 1515, Abby's room. Abby had the foresight for each of them to keep a copy of the other's room key. "Just in case," he remembered her telling him.

He pressed his ear against the door and listened for a few seconds before drawing his weapon and entering the room. It was empty, but he spotted Abby's shoulder bag right away. He holstered the small Sig P239, his weapon of choice when traveling, and checked that the laptop was still inside. It was.

Kang powered up the device, eager to plug in the answer they had received from the young girl at the Sky Bar. If the people behind the game were responsible for the attack, he wanted to send a message that they were still playing the game and that it would take more than a street fight to stop them.

Once the game loaded and the paper scroll unraveled, Kang punched in the phrase *The Big Mango*.

A few seconds later, the paper scroll unraveled further and revealed their task.

Indulge in your favorite forbidden fruit.

It was obvious to Kang that the task called for the player to kill one of the many women or men who hired out their services. *Sickening*, he thought to himself.

He shut the computer down, slipped it back in the shoulder bag, and headed for his original room. Kang took the same precautions before entering as he had done with Abby's room. He still believed someone could be watching him or, worse, setting up for another attack. Kang quickly changed into his own clothing and grabbed his passport from the hotel safe. Everything else he left untouched.

Chapter 33

I woke up with a dull throbbing near the base of my skull and quickly concluded that a blow to my head had knocked me out. It was the only explanation I could think of that would have me waking up in what seemed to be a park—a dark park, I might add.

I sat up and felt relatively okay, except for my head. None of my limbs appeared to be broken, and the best discovery yet was that I had been lying on my purse. Inside, I found my wallet. However, my brand new cell phone, my weapon and the three thousand baht, roughly a hundred dollars, I had in my wallet were gone. No surprise there, but at least I still had my ATM and credit cards.

I sat up and started piecing together the events of the night from the moment we had left the Sky Bar to the fight on the street to the conversation with the masked man. That last one still felt like it never really happened, but it had. How else could I explain waking up under a tree? At the moment, I had more questions than I did answers.

Was there trouble in gameland? Why else would they reach out to us? Is it just Bangkok, or are they having trouble in all the cities? Could the game really be unraveling? But the most pressing question in my mind was, if the man or men behind the game knew that Kang and I weren't the real Carlsons, why let us continue to play the game? *What do they have to gain from it? How long have they known?*

I didn't know the answer, but I figured if they controlled the game, they determined what information we received. *They're in control. They've always been in control. And now they're using us to fix a problem.*

I couldn't be sure whether Kang had escaped the ambush or if he, too, had been taken and later released. I wished those men hadn't taken my phone; I could have at least called him or checked to see if he had tried to reach me. With our identities compromised, I knew Kang would make his way back to the safe location we had set up. And that's exactly where I intended to go.

Off in the distance, I saw a line of streetlights—a road. If I could reach that area, I would be able to flag a cab, or so I hoped. My eyesight had adjusted fairly quickly to the dark. I could make out the trees and bushes around me, so I didn't think I would have trouble navigating. However, there was one problem I wasn't prepared for—the hissing I heard nearby.

Still on my knees, I spun around and saw a shadowy, four-legged creature with a long tail approaching me. It hissed again just as it came out from the shadows of the tree and into the moonlight. It was a large monitor lizard, and it was heading my way.

I popped to my feet faster than a kernel of corn hitting hot oil and took off for the highway. I looked back and saw that the mini-dragon was fast on my heels. *What the hell is that thing doing in a park?* I had no idea, but it looked hungry.

Adrenaline raced through my body, moving my tiny legs at the speed of blur, or at least that's the speed I hoped to be moving at. I had kicked off my sandals after my first few strides and continued barefoot.

My heart thumped against my chest almost immediately. Sweat rained down my face and neck. The humidity in the air had begun its assault. All at once, it seemed like my clothes soaked up a bathtub of water and clung to my body like fresh papier-mâché, but I had no intention of slowing down and becoming that lizard's late-night snack.

With the reptile quickly gaining on me, I knew I had to throw that guy a curve ball or something close to it. I tried running in a zigzag course, hoping it didn't have the agility to pivot while running. Wrong. It pivoted just fine.

I must have sounded the alarm, because out of the corner of my eye, I saw another lizard scurrying toward me. *What the hell?* I had always thought these lizards were vegetarians, happy to eat fruits and vegetables. At least, that's what I had always seen them eating in the zoo. Maybe they were opportunists and took advantage of sick or dead animals. Did I really look worse than I felt?

I watched the scaly creature to my right close in on me. It had an angle that would put him on course for a collision with my legs.

Without thought, my years of training from running the 110-meter hurdles as a teenager instinctively came back. I put my head down and focused on my own timing. At the right moment, I leaped. My left leg shot out in front, and my right foot bent at the knee as my arms powered me forward. I sailed over the confused creature.

My form was dead-on for someone wearing jeans and clutching a small purse. I stuck my landing, and my legs continued to propel me forward. Up ahead, another lizard appeared, and I sailed effortlessly over that one as well. That night, I was leapin' lizards.

As I neared the road and the streetlights got brighter, I looked behind me and saw that the trio of lizards had backed off. I didn't slow, though, and kept my pace until my feet hit the hard sidewalk. I took another peek behind and did not see them. They had disappeared. *What kind of park lets five-foot-long lizards roam their grounds?*

I continued, barefoot, along the sidewalk, looking for a taxi. My clothes were drenched with sweat, and I was still breathing hard. From what I could tell, the only other people out here at this time of the night were working. Most of the streetwalkers I passed were ladyboys, but these ladyboys didn't look much like ladies. They stared but said nothing as

I passed them by. I didn't feel threatened, confident I could take any one of them on, perhaps even two at once.

One of them approached me cautiously. My guard was up, reasonable if you ask me, considering the night I'd had.

The ladyboy spoke with a heavy accent. "You okay?"

"I'm fine. Could you tell me where I am?"

"Lumpini Park. You want cab?"

"Yes. I need to go to Sukhumvit, near the Terminal 21 shopping center."

She motioned for me to stop and walked to the edge of the sidewalk. One of her heels buckled, but she quickly righted herself and flagged a taxi. She opened the back door and said something in Thai before looking back at me. "Okay, he take you, but must pay 200b. No meter."

At that point, I didn't care if I overpaid, and I nodded that it was fine. I knew I had no money on me, but ATMs were abundant. The cabbie would have no choice but to wait and trust that I wouldn't skip out on the fare. Worst-case scenario, I pull out my FBI badge and pull rank on the poor guy.

Chapter 34

I exited the cab a block before the Sheraton hotel. I had hidden the key card to the room in a pebble garden near the hotel's entrance. I waited for a few hotel guests to pass me by before bending down and digging under some rocks. The card was still there, and a wave of relief moved through my body.

My blouse remained stuck to my chest and back, and my jeans had a fair share of grass stains on them, but other than that, I didn't think I would draw any attention unless someone noticed I wasn't wearing shoes. But this was Bangkok; I was sure the hotel staff saw people wander through the lobby in all sorts of dress. I walked steadily to the elevator, avoiding eye contact with anyone and headed up to the twentieth floor.

When I reached the room, I stood outside the door for a minute listening. I didn't have a weapon, so I was apprehensive about barging in, even though I knew the location was safe. I inserted the card key into the slot and slowly opened the door. The lights were on from the night's turndown service, but the room itself was empty. I closed the door behind me and looked for any signs that Kang might have made it to the location before I did, but I saw nothing.

I moved over to the hotel phone and dialed Kang's cell. All I got was voicemail. I left a message saying I was at the restaurant. At the moment, all I could do was hope Kang had survived our attack and was making his way back to the location. I also had no way to get a hold of Artie. I had tossed his card after punching his phone number into my cell, which I didn't have.

When we checked into the hotel, I'd had the clarity of mind to stash a bag containing a change of clothes in the room. I had asked Kang if he'd wanted to do the same, but he said he could do without it; to each his own. I took a shower and changed into fresh jeans and a T-shirt.

Afterward, I put a call into Reilly to update him on the situation. As usual, he wanted to send reinforcements. He even broached the subject of pulling me out.

"Abby, this is serious. You have a member of the SFPD unaccounted for, he could be dead for all we know, and now there's a bounty on your head."

"Calm down. We don't know that. Kang's a tough guy. I'm sure he's alive somewhere."

"What makes you so sure of that?"

"The men that attacked us, as far as I can tell, need us. It's the only reason I can see why they would alert us that another team is targeting us. They could have let it play out and enjoyed the outcome, but they didn't. Something's wrong."

Reilly remained quiet on the line for a brief second before speaking again. "Okay, Abby. You've got twelve hours. If after that the situation still remains the same, I'm pulling you out. I'll have to alert Detective Kang's superiors about the situation. I can't control what they will do, but I'll encourage them to give you time. Hopefully they'll have as much confidence in their guy as I do in you."

I thanked Reilly for the extra time and hung up. My next thought was to track down Artie by seeking help from his precinct in Thong Lo.

I was about to leave when I heard a noise outside the door. I hit the lights and hid myself inside the closet near the room door. *Is that Kyle?* The closet door had slats. The levers pointed down, so I had some visibility. There was a flashlight hanging from the wall right above the hotel safe. It felt heavy enough to use as a club.

I heard more movement outside the door and then a key card being inserted into the lock mechanism. A beat later, the door opened and the light from the hallway poured into the room. A shadowy figure entered, though because of my short stature, I could only see the bottom half of the person for a brief moment before the door closed and the room went dark. That was my opportunity.

I shoved the door open, hoping I had timed it right and it would slam into whoever had entered. My timing seemed okay, because I heard a grunt and the sound of someone falling to the floor. I exited the closet and backed away while switching the flashlight on. Sitting on his butt and propped up by one arm was Kang, and he had a bloody nose.

Chapter 35

"What the hell?" Kang cried out after I had switched on one of the lamps in the room.

"I'm sorry. I had to take precautions. I'm unarmed," I said as I moved his hand away from his nose. "It doesn't look broken." I grabbed a towel from the bathroom and handed it to him. "Do you want me to get some ice? I'm sure there's a machine, or room service can—"

"I'm fine." He got up and took a seat on the bed. He pulled the towel away from his nose and looked at it.

I felt a little bad for the guy, but I didn't regret looking out for myself. I grabbed two bottles of water from the mini-bar and handed one to Kang. "Use it as an ice pack."

Kang removed the towel and placed the bottle against his nose for few seconds before deciding it wasn't really helping.

"The bleeding seems to have stopped," I said as I took a seat in a chair.

"Bleeding nose aside, I'm really glad to see that you're okay, Abby, but didn't you see my note?" He walked over to the desk. "Hmm, well, I left a message here for you. I guess the maid thought it was trash."

"I glad you're okay, too. Sorry about the nose."

Kang cracked a smile while waving a dismissive hand. We updated each other while he dabbed at his bloody nostrils.

"We're an actual task for this Creeper guy?" His response came muffled through the towel.

"His goal is to deliver us dead in a creative way."

"Good luck," Kang said with an eye roll. "I'll kick that guy's ass from here to Timbuktu."

"My thoughts exactly, but I think this masked man, mastermind or not, realizes this. I think they believe we'll be the ones to prevail. They want this guy either locked up or dead. I'm sure dead is their preference."

"He must have pissed off someone big time to get ratted on like this," Kang said as he pulled the towel away from his nose once again before cracking the seal on his bottle of water and taking a sip.

"You know what keeps getting stuck in my mind?" I asked while leaning forward. "Why us? If he broke a rule or isn't playing the game right or whatever, why not just ban him or freeze his account?"

"Good question."

"We're not bounty hunters. Our goal is to catch him and lock him up, not kill him."

"Maybe they're hoping it goes down that way. This is a sick individual we're dealing with. He could be one of those maniacs that chooses to go out fighting rather than give up."

I nodded and scratched at the side of my head.

"You think this masked man you had a conversation with is the mastermind behind the game?" Kang asked.

I pursed my lips while I thought about his question. "I don't think he's the main guy. But he could be a person who manages the players in the city. I mean, one person can't keep track of what's happening in every city, at least not on a hands-on level. Someone has to manage the players when they come to town. My thought is they have men in place in each city. Jing Woo in San Francisco. This guy in Bangkok."

"Makes sense to have people running the game on a local level."

"Makes a lot of sense," I agreed. "Maybe something went wrong on this guy's watch, and he's trying to fix it? Maybe he heard what happened to Jing. I wouldn't be surprised if it was the mastermind that had Jing taken out and not an enemy."

"That could be their safety catch. Something goes wrong, they eliminate their guys on the ground and shut down the game in the city."

"It creates a dead end."

Kang dabbed the towel at his nose a few more times before setting it aside. "If this masked man is the guy in charge of managing the game here, surely he's capable of doing it himself. No need to involve us."

"He might be doing that."

"So what? We're the backup plan?"

"Either that, or he needs us to keep playing the game. Maybe he doesn't want to take the chance that the Creeper gets to us."

Kang leaned back in his chair and ran his hand across his mouth and chin. "There's something definitely wrong if he needs us to keep playing. We're the law."

I thought for a moment about what Kang had said. The men behind the game knew who we were, yet they still engaged us. I really didn't know what to make of the situation at the time. They were trying to use us as a pawn in their twisted game. That wasn't something I was keen on letting happen unless it proved to be useful to our investigation.

We sat quietly rehashing our conversation. It was then that I realized that Kang had never finished telling me about his conversation with Artie.

"You're right. I called Artie as soon as I could and told him about the attack. By the time we met up at Terminal 21, he had already sent some of his men to the area to question the street vendors. After we spoke, he said he was heading over there to help."

"Anything else?"

"Yeah," Kang said with a surprised laugh. "They found the body that was used to make the human som tum."

"Anything interesting about the victim?"

"He said she was a dancer at two bars. He talked to the

mama-sans at both locations, and one remembered seeing this Creeper guy but couldn't provide anything more than a matching description."

"It seems as though everyone who sees him remembers him. That's got to give us an edge on finding him. I wonder if he's targeting working women."

"Bar girls are easy targets. They're willing to come with you which eliminates the need for any abduction," Kang said.

"There's that, but I am wondering if it's more about the power that comes with hiring someone. Does he like women he can control?" I stood and walked over to the large picture window and stared out at the city for a moment before facing Kang again. "The control, the sex… it can all feed his desires."

"So this guy would be seeking out these type of women, game or no game."

"I think so."

"So what's the reason to come after us? We won't fulfill his needs."

"My thoughts exactly. Whether he's been tasked to kill us or not, the real question is, would he even bother?" The more I thought about what I had just said, the more I kept nodding my head. I was beginning to think the Creeper wouldn't come after us.

That's when I realized I might be asking the wrong question. "Maybe it's not about us. Maybe it's about them.

What do the gamekeepers have to gain from having the Creeper taken out?"

Kang smiled. "That's the best question yet."

"The game is in trouble. It has to be. To what degree, I don't know but that's got to be it."

I tried to give it more thought, but Kang's yawning had finally caught up to me.

"It's late," he said, looking at his watch. "We should try to get some sleep."

I agreed. *A little shut-eye might bring a bit more clarity.*

The room we were in had two twin beds, so I didn't have to tell Kang that we weren't sharing one. I might have shared it though—strictly for sleeping. I had become comfortable around him. And I thought he was cute in a goofy way. He was nothing like the men I usually dated, which made it even harder to grasp why I had a crush on the guy.

Chapter 36

The shy girl couldn't believe her good fortune. A handsome man—a handsome farang, at that—had shown interest in her. He had chosen to sit next to her and buy her a drink. Not one, but two. It thrilled her and fed her ego. Some of the dancers from inside the bar had come out to the patio to see whom the farang had chosen. She was quick to sit up proudly and let them take notice.

Having arrived in Bangkok from Surin, in the northeastern region of Thailand, over a year ago for a job at a computer company, Ly had only been working at the club for a little over a month. Her initial job simply didn't pay as well as she had hoped it would. At least, it wouldn't until she remained there for at least five years. That was too long for someone who had a family of four back home relying on her for financial support.

Through a mutual friend, Ly had met a go-go dancer, Mai, who worked at Soi Cowboy, and she spent an afternoon talking to the girl. Ly thought the dancer's life was exciting, considering Ly often didn't have much money to go out after meeting her obligations.

"It's fun," Mai said. "I can work whenever I want, and

I make good money."

"You like dancing?" Ly asked.

Mai shrugged her shoulders. "It's okay. At first I was shy, but now it's better. I try to sit with a customer and have fun so they will bar fine me right away, then I don't have to dance."

"What's a bar fine?"

"It's the money a man must pay the bar if they want me. It releases me from having to dance. I can do whatever I want with them after they pay."

"So if they bar fine you, what? You just talk to them?"

"Sure, and we have drinks."

"But you go with them?" Ly asked. Her eyes darted away quickly, worried that her question might be too personal.

But the dancer didn't have a problem discussing the details of her job. "Yeah, if they're not crazy," she said with a laugh. "I go with them short-time. I don't like long-time."

Ly tilted her head and scrunched her eyebrows. "Why?"

"If I go short-time, I can come back to the club after and bar fine again. I make more money this way."

"Really? That fast?"

"Sure. Sometimes it only takes twenty minutes at the hotel and I'm on my way back. Some men only thirty seconds," she said, laughing. "I only go long-time if they take me for a full day, not just overnight."

Mai went on to tell her about the men that had taken her on trips and shopping sprees and had even given her an allowance. This was all on top of the money she made from the bar from dancing and through lady drinks. Ly couldn't believe it.

"You're very pretty," Mai said as she fingered a strand of Ly's hair. "You could get a job at the bar, and many customers would want you."

Ly didn't believe her, but Mai convinced her to come to the bar and see for herself. She desperately needed the money but was still apprehensive about working at a bar. It meant having sex with men. Though she thought it couldn't hurt to go see what it was all about and agreed to meet Mai.

The following night, Mai sat Ly down at a table outside the bar. "I'll start you off with your first drink," she said. "I promise you will have a customer sitting with you really soon, but you cannot leave with them. You don't work here yet." Mai then headed inside.

Ly sat quietly amongst the other reception girls and sipped her drink. It didn't take long for a nice gentleman to sit with her and buy her another drink. She started to have fun, and before she knew it, she had spent the entire night talking and drinking with different men. All of them were interested in taking her back to their hotel room. The test run had been successful.

Later, she had a short talk with the mama-san and was hired as a reception girl. She would earn fifty baht for every lady drink, and men could bar fine her if they wanted. On top of that, she got a monthly salary of eight thousand baht a month. Her computer job paid only twelve thousand baht. Between the bar salary and drinks alone, Ly felt confident she could easily make the same amount and have fun doing it. And if she did go with men, she figured she could make double, maybe even more.

By the time she had encountered the handsome farang that warm summer night, Ly had already gone with a number of men to their hotels. So when the farang smiled and ran his hand through his blond hair before asking if she would come back to his hotel, the answer was an easy yes.

Everything had gone as planned that night. After a few drinks, Ly left the bar with her prize. He had a suite at the Westin, only a block away. They had agreed to a short-time arrangement, but later, while she lay in the afterglow of delicious sex, he asked if she would spend the night. Ly happily said yes and fell asleep in his arms.

The next day, she joined him for breakfast in the hotel restaurant, and that was when he inquired about her spending the next seven days with him. Ly's eyes widened. It was her first, real long-time proposition. "Sure," she said. "Where do you want to go?"

He told her they had to stay in Bangkok this time. He had to work but wanted company. Sure, the prospect of taking a trip somewhere excited her, and she was a little disappointed with his answer, but she would make five thousand baht a day for seven days, and that easily made up for it.

Though she would regret this decision on the second day.

Chapter 37

Somchai's men stood silently around his desk as he struggled to contain his anger. He gritted his teeth and gripped his fists tightly as he looked at each and every one of them. They, of course, avoided any eye contact with their boss. None wanted to be the one to set him off. An uncontrolled outburst could cause him to lose face—to be embarrassed to the point of shame. One of them would surely be eliminated should that happened. It would be the only way for Somchai to regain their respect again.

For the time being, the room remained silent. Only the hum of the air conditioning unit attached to the wall seemed brave enough to make its presence known. Eventually, Somchai calmed himself enough to address his men. "Why can't you find him?"

Nobody spoke. Somchai asked again. This time his tone elevated slightly.

A tall, skinny man finally answered Somchai's question. "We've asked all over. No one has seen the farang with a limp," he said.

"You are sure you have searched everywhere?"

"We have been everywhere."

Somchai still didn't understand. What could possibly
be so hard about finding an ugly farang with a limp? He
would stick out. Surely a vendor or a motortaxi driver
would have seen him around. Somchai still believed that the
Creeper was somewhere in the Sukhumvit area and ordered
his men to continue looking.

A day and a half had already passed since he had
spoken to the mastermind. He knew he had another day or
so before he would receive a call asking why Team Creeper
had not initiated the second Attraction. What then? What
could he say that would buy him time? The truth was not
possible. He had already crossed the line and withheld
information. To do so would cause the mastermind to lose
face. Somchai would pay for it in ways that made him
shudder just thinking about it.

Somchai knew his men were speaking the truth when
they said they could not find the Creeper, and that troubled
him. They knew the area well and all of the shop owners,
food vendors, and taxi drivers. It was virtually impossible
for anyone to go unnoticed in the area, and yet the Creeper
had. Had he forced himself to stay indoors? Even so, the
owner of the hotel or condo would know he was there. Had
he left Bangkok and traveled to another city, or worse, to
another country? Possibly, but someone would have seen
him on the street. A taxi driver would have taken him to the
airport or the train station.

Somchai's anger bubbled again. His right leg bounced

uncontrollably while he envisioned multiple scenarios of how his situation might play out—none of them ideal. With his men gone leaving him alone with his thoughts, his imagination only fueled the one-sided conversation he had begun. Somchai had suddenly found himself in the most unlikely of predicaments, one he had thought would never happen to him.

Somchai had spent years working for the secret Chinese organization. This was unbelievable to most of its members since Somchai was only half Chinese. His other half was Thai. All of his counterparts who held a position of power within the organization were of pure Chinese descent, but Somchai had proven himself worthy and was rewarded with control over the Chinatown in Bangkok.

Chinatown was nowhere near the touristy Sukhumvit area. It was located on Yarowat Street in the Samphanthawong district near the Grand Palace. As with every Chinatown, no matter the country, the walls that surrounded it were impenetrable by anyone who wasn't Chinese. The Thai police had no jurisdiction in the area— not because they didn't want it. They did, but they couldn't obtain it. They had been strong-armed out of the area. It didn't help that the Thai government never bothered to push the issue because the right officials were receiving the right amount of baht every month to keep it that way.

Still, the issue caused Somchai to fume. *What did I do wrong? I did nothing*, he thought. The Creeper had broken the rules of the game and had forced his hand. He had no choice but to react the way he did. The farang was the one responsible for the mess. And now Somchai feared he would take the blame for it.

Maybe the FBI agent and the detective will catch him. Somchai knew that at that point he was grasping. He had started to regret his decision to involve those two. Or did he? He didn't know. It seemed he had second-guessed every decision he had made since the Creeper arrived in Bangkok. One minute, he patted himself on the back; the next, he cursed his own actions.

Somchai stood and started pacing, still continuing the conversation with himself.

You fool. You've ruined everything.

Me? It was that farang. He did this.

You should have prevented it. You should have watched him closer.

How? Have him live with me?

You're in charge of the game in Bangkok. You must control the players.

He should never have been invited to the game.

Somchai spent the next half hour arguing with himself. His hands emphasized both sides of the conversation as he stood in front of his desk, staring at the empty chair behind it. He could have continued for another half hour if it had not been for the knocking.

Somchai opened the door to find one of his men

standing outside. His eyes were wide and his breaths short. In his hand, he held a tablet. Somchai glanced at the screen and saw that he had the game up and running.

"What is it?" he asked.

"Team Creeper. He's... He's activated the second Attraction."

Chapter 38

I woke the following morning at a little after seven. With his back still facing me, Kang had his blanket wrapped tightly around his body. In Dreamland I supposed. I knew I would have to wake him soon, but I figured I'd let him catch a few more snores while I slipped out and got us some breakfast.

When I returned to the room twenty minutes later, I found Kang dressed and sitting in front of the laptop with the blackout curtains drawn open. He had yet to tame his bed head, sporting an off-kilter Mohawk. I figured he was checking email or looking at the game, but oh, how wrong I was.

"Kyle," a woman's voice whined. "Don't you miss me? You were supposed to call me every day."

Oh, you have got to be kidding me. I peeked at the screen and saw that Kang was Skyping with my nemesis, Suzi Zhang.

I placed a cup of coffee and a breakfast sandwich next him but said nothing, even though I could clearly hear her going on and on about how everyone in San Francisco was so happy that she had returned to anchor the nightly news. I knew for fact she was lying, because I wasn't happy to see her plastic face on my television screen.

I took a seat on my bed and tried to ignore her, but my ears were kept wax-free and shutting her out was impossible. To top things off, all I had to drink was prepackaged green tea. My tin of loose-leaf, unfortunately, was back in my old room, and I had no choice but to stomach the generic stuff. I unwrapped the teabag and dunked it into my cup of hot water, wondering how long their conversation would continue. Fortunately, Kang had the presence of mind to end it quickly.

"Sorry about that," he said, flashing me a crooked grin from his seat.

"Everything okay?" I asked, not really wanting to know the answer.

"Yeah." Kang waved his hand at me. "Just checking in. You know…"

"Yeah."

He turned to face me. "I heard you leave earlier, so I thought I should get up." He must have noticed me wincing when I took a sip. "Slumming with prepackaged tea, huh?"

I didn't want to chuckle, but he was right.

"By the way, thanks for this." He unwrapped his sandwich and took a bite.

"So last night, you mentioned right before we turned in that you had unlocked the next task," I said.

"I did. 'Indulge in your favorite forbidden fruit,'" he

said between quick chews. "Any immediate thoughts on the riddle?"

"Something sexual?" I grabbed my sandwich and unwrapped it.

"Those were my thoughts: Kill one of the many sex workers in Bangkok. Thinking about it makes my stomach turn."

"Why's that?" I asked before taking a bite. "The other tasks didn't seem to affect you."

Kang's shoulders bounced once. "Eh, I think it's because I've gotten to know some of the workers back in San Francisco. They're my best source for what's happening on the streets."

"And...?"

"They're normal people, just like you and me. I can't help but think that the reason for targeting them is that the people creating the tasks think they're disposable."

"I don't think these a-holes put that much thought into who is targeted."

"Yeah, I know that's not the reason, but it's stuck in my head."

I chewed quietly as I thought about the task. We needed to keep it simple and connected to someone in the sex business. "You know, I don't think we need to do the whole crime scene thing anymore."

A muffled grunt came from Kang's busy mouth.

"It's never really played a role in our advancement to

the next Attraction. All the mastermind cares about is how creative we get with the kill."

"And you said the investigation Artie performed was low-key. That it didn't have an effect in closing out the first Bangkok Attraction."

"Nope. Speaking of, we need to get a hold of Artie."

Kang shoved the rest of his sandwich into his mouth and mumbled, "I have his number saved on this disposable."

"What happened to your phone?"

"I think I lost it while playing motorbike daredevil."

Kang called Artie and made arrangements for the detective to meet us at the Starbucks where we'd first met. We both agreed that Artie didn't need to know we were staying at a new location. But he did need to be made aware of something very important: If we were being targeted, then we had to assume he was also.

Chapter 39

We arrived at the coffee shop first, as I'd expected we would; it was only a fifteen-minute walk from our new location. I secured a table in the back corner for privacy while Kang fetched us some drinks. I took the opportunity to text the kids from his phone. If my math was right, they should have been finishing with dinner. When I wasn't at home, Po Po took it upon herself to slide the time from 6:00 p.m. to 5:30 p.m. So long as the kids ate, it didn't bother me what time they chowed down. I just didn't like having to rush home from work every night just to eat with everyone.

Ryan responded first. His judo class had been cancelled because of a water leak at the dojo, so he had spent the afternoon finishing his homework and reading. What more could I ask for? Lucy, on the other hand, told me she had watched TV all afternoon. I again had to remind Po Po to be more aware of the time Lucy's butt spent parked in front of the TV. For a strong woman, she sure could be weak at times.

Over the last year, Lucy had developed her "sad look." She had gotten the idea from *Shrek*'s Puss in Boots—and it made the old woman cave every single time. I told my mother-in-law repeatedly that she needed to be tough and not let it bother her. "She isn't really sad. You know that, right?"

Of course, Lucy's act didn't cut it with me. I would shut the TV off after her allotted thirty minutes were up without warning. She would cry and say, "But don't you love me, Mommy?" Sure, on the inside I was dying and wanted to snatch her up in my arms as she produced the most adorable pout on the planet, but I didn't. On the outside, I was cold stone—Tiger Mom.

I sent a few more texts and then turned the mobile back over to Kang when he returned so he could message you-know-who. We only stopped texting when Artie seemed to appear out of nowhere.

"Abby. Kyle."

We both looked up to see the smiling detective walking toward us.

"Do you want a coffee?" Kang offered.

Artie shook his head. "I'm fine." He sat in the chair next to Kang. "Abby, I'm glad you're okay. You had me worried."

"Just a little kidnapping. Nothing too big." I filled Artie in on what had happened.

"Wait. You're telling me the men behind the game kidnapped you so they could help us catch the other player in town?"

"It appears that way. The masked man didn't come

outright and say that, but it was obvious he played some sort of significant role."

"So your cover is blown." Artie turned both palms up. "How long do you think they have known?"

"My guess is they knew all along." I pressed my mug against my lips.

"So it's over. That's it." Artie brushed his hands together.

"Not necessarily. If these men knew Kyle and I weren't the real Team Carlson, why let us continue to play the game? They could have cut us off at any time."

"Instead, they've turned this Creeper guy loose on you two."

"Don't discount yourself. We have to assume we're all a target."

Artie nodded in agreement. "So this arrangement is their idea of fun? They want to see who will win?"

"That's one way to look at it."

"But you think it's something else?"

"I do," I said, leaning back in my chair. This man risked a lot by attacking us and confronting me personally. What makes the game successful is the fact that no one knows who's behind it."

"Well, I've got news that can help us further unmask this man. My men were able to find a vendor who fingered one of your attackers."

"Just like that?" Kang mentioned.

"My guys can be convincing."

I'm sure a closed-off room with no cameras helped.

"We're looking for a low-level Triad gang member," Artie continued. "He hangs around Chinatown. Once we pick him up, we should be able to get him to tell us what he knows." Artie smiled a smile that could convey only one thing—more closed-off rooms with no cameras.

I brought up the problem of my missing weapon. I could replace my cell with a disposable like Kang had, but securing a proper handgun was a larger issue.

"Can't your liaison at the embassy help you out with that?" Kang asked. "You have to report that it's missing, right?"

"Yes and yes, but I'm a little hesitant about involving him just yet. I want to get Reilly's advice first."

"If it helps, I can arrange to get you a weapon," Artie said with a shrug.

Kang and I looked at each other before looking back at Artie. He took that as a yes and wrote down the name of a man at his station that I should see. "Give me two days to organize this. If you need it, it'll be available."

"Thanks. This is helpful."

Artie smiled. "In the meantime, the two of you should lie low until I can get my hands on the guy who attacked you."

Chapter 40

Before we parted ways, Artie offered to position a few men outside the Landmark Plaza. A nice gesture, but since we weren't staying there, we declined. "We don't want the attention," Kang said.

I, on the other hand, wasn't comfortable with the idea of waiting around. After Artie left, I turned to Kang. "There's no way we're sitting put until he produces this guy."

"My thoughts exactly. Go after the Creeper?"

"It's the only thing that makes sense. We've got a decent description of the guy. He's bound to show up at Nana Plaza or Soi Cowboy."

"You think he'll disregard the task given him—you know, to come after us?"

"Not necessarily. But he'll certainly prioritize. This city is like a candy store to him. There's an endless supply of the right type of women to fulfill his desires. He'll take full advantage of the situation and feed as much as he can."

"Well, first things first; we need to get you a weapon and a phone."

Two days later, I was equipped with an unregistered Glock. I expected a lot of red tape, but the man Artie told us to see didn't require my signature or any information. I told him who I was, and he handed me a shopping bag. Inside, I saw a firearm, a holster and a box of ammunition. That was it. Talk about low-key. Had I followed protocol and gone to my liaison at the embassy, I would instead be facing an inquiry about my missing weapon before anyone talked about replacing it. Reilly also knew that would have happened, which is why I had received his blessing.

The weapon was an older model that had seen better days. The handle had a small dent, but the piece looked to be in working condition. Nonetheless, Kang and I picked up supplies so I could properly clean the gun before we searched out a shooting range. It worked.

By then, we had moved all of our belongings out of the Landmark Plaza and over to the Sheraton. We debated whether we really needed to stay at the new location. Over the course of the last couple days, we had learned enough about the Creeper to know who we were dealing with. That had lessened the "unknown" factor for us, but still, why take the chance? We had a target on our backs. No sense in enlarging it.

While waiting on my weapon, Kang had picked up a tourist map of Bangkok so we could begin making plans to track the Creeper down before he got to us.

We marked both Nana Plaza and Soi Cowboy as hot spots. Nana was a ten-minute walk from our hotel; Cowboy was less than five. We knew that, between those two locations, working women could be found in a bunch of bars, not to mention the sidewalk bars that popped up at night and the lobbies of most hotels. The Creeper had a lot of places he could go, and we couldn't be in all places at once. We'd have to hedge our bets that he would troll the two entertainment centers.

"You know," Kang started, "you could pass for a Thai, especially if you did that eye makeup thing they all seem to do." He gestured vaguely to the outer corner of his eyes.

I knew what Kang was talking about. Since arriving in Bangkok, I had noticed that the women here applied their eyeliner in a very specific way; they drew it out to a point near the outer corners of their eyes. It was very characteristic of their look, but that's not what he was really trying to say. "You want me to pose as a working girl?"

He shrugged. "Makes complete sense, considering where we'll be. You might be the Creeper's type. I can pose as a customer."

"Why not pose as girlfriend and boyfriend?"

"You yourself said the Creeper has a fetish for working women."

Kang was right. Posing as a bargirl would be the best approach, but I would most definitely draw the line at getting up on a stage and shaking my behind.

Once we had a plan in place, I popped over to the Terminal 21 shopping center for makeup and an appropriate outfit. I ended up purchasing a black cocktail dress, a pair of heels and a clutch.

When I returned to the room, I showed off my new look to Kang and got the thumbs up.

"Wow, you look hot!" Kang blurted. Immediately afterward his face turned beet-red. "I mean you did a fine job of mimicking that look."

"Really?" I said as I headed back into the bathroom for another look in the mirror.

"Yeah, the makeup is dead-on," I heard Kang call out.

"Is that what you're wearing?" I asked as I exited the bathroom.

Kang nodded. "Why?"

He wore tan cargo shorts and a blue short-sleeved shirt, which worked. Most of the men we saw walking around town were dressed very casually. "It's a good look," I said. "You look just like a tourist."

Kang smiled. "A customer," he corrected as he gave me the thumbs up.

Chapter 41

We chose the closer venue, Soi Cowboy, for our stakeout that night. We arrived at the location a little after eight. The soi already had a good crowd of men milling about, and the hostesses for each bar were hard at work cajoling as many men as they could into their respective establishments.

The plan changed when we got there. It dawned on us that I wouldn't be able to sit at a bar and pretend to be a working girl. The mama-sans would chase me off the premises in heartbeat if they knew a lady not associated with the bar was trying to work their territory, so to speak. Kang was now my date, and it wouldn't matter if I were working or not.

Ideally, I would sit there by myself with a team of agents watching me, but we didn't have access to that type of support, at least not without involving Artie. We had to make do and hope we could spot the Creeper.

We walked the length of the soi slowly before doubling back and sitting at an outdoor table in front of a bar called Tilac. We ordered a round of drinks and kept an eye out for our guy.

Twenty minutes had passed before I leaned in closer to Kang. "I'm not so sure this is the best possible use of our time. I mean, if we knew the Creeper frequented this bar, then yeah, but we don't."

Kang nodded in agreement. "You're right. This guy could be anywhere. Ideally, we would have a few teams here and over at Nana Plaza. And even then, it could take a couple days, if we were lucky, for this guy to show up."

I sat quietly, swirling the last of the Jameson in my glass. The men passing by in front of me all had large smiles stretched across their faces. Their heads swiveled from side to side like they were watching a tennis match. They looked to be in their early forties and up and were an even mix of Asian and Caucasian tourists and businessmen. What I saw got me thinking.

"Take a look at the men here," I said. "What do you see?"

Kang looked up and down the soi. "What do you mean? They're guys."

"The men here are older, dressed well. A lot appear to be businessmen. They have money."

"What are you getting at?" Kang asked.

"The game. There's a lot of travel involved. That takes money, a lot of money."

"Rich killers?"

I swallowed the last of my drink. "They have to have some sort of decent cash flow coming in to support themselves."

Kang shifted in his seat to face me. "I still don't know where you're heading with this line of thought."

I tapped the table with my finger. "Our old hotel was closer to Nana Plaza. I noticed that the men around that area looked different than the men here."

"They looked more budget-conscious," Kang added, his head tilted to the side.

"Exactly. If we assume our Creeper guy has money, he might be more prone to come to this location. The women are younger here and much more beautiful, which means they cost a lot more."

"So you think we can cross off Nana and focus on this place based on the theory that men with money tend to come here."

"It's a way to start narrowing it down."

I watched Kang scratch at his chin, something he always did when he wasn't sure if he agreed with me or not.

"You're not buying it," I said.

"Feels like a stretch. If we had a little history on his victims, it might help—Wait a minute. Artie mentioned the bar his victim might have worked at."

"Do you remember the name?"

Kang kept scratching. "I think one of them was called the Shag Bar."

"Shag?"

"Or maybe it was Shark."

"Well, we can quickly see if either of those bars are here."

We got up and walked the soi again.

"There," Kang pointed at a neon sign with a large blue shark. The word "Shark" burned brightly above it.

To be sure there wasn't a bar called Shag, we finished our loop of the soi. A few minutes later, we were sitting inside the Shark bar.

The venue itself had the typical lighting and the thumping bass of a nightclub. There were two levels of seating around a small stage where fifteen women were shaking away. I saw a couple of empty seats on the second level in the corner. Perfect for us. We had an unobstructed view of the bar entrance and most of the seating area.

I took my time letting my eyes wander the room, but I didn't see anyone who fit the description of our guy. I looked at my watch; the night was young, only 9:30 p.m.

Kang motioned with his chin to the other side of the room. "I see dancers making their way up and down the stairs. There might be a second level, maybe even a third. I'll go check it out, make sure our guy isn't already up there."

After Kang left, I fell into a trance watching the women on stage. They wore white, see-through bikini tops and matching skirts that were no longer than four inches, allowing the bottom of their G-stringed cheeks to show. Half of the dancers seemed to be into the music and were making a gallant effort at moving their bodies in a sexy-dance way, while the other half appeared bored and couldn't wait for their time on stage to be up so they could sit next to a man or with their friends.

I wondered; if I were their age, would I have the balls to get up on stage half-naked to dance for men? I imagine that, for some, it felt empowering, but if I had to guess, the rest of them viewed it as nothing more than a job.

I continued to watch the women while sipping Jameson out of my cocktail glass. It wasn't until he said, "Hello," that I realized a man with blond hair and a charming smile stood next to me.

"Is this seat taken?" he asked.

Chapter 42

I was a little taken back by the stranger who seemed to appear out of nowhere. There were other seats available. Why sit next to me? Better yet, why not sit closer to the stage? I scooted over a bit and, in the process realized why he sat next to me. *Dress. Makeup. Got it.*

He continued to smile when I crossed my legs, so I returned the pleasantry. He then leaned over and asked my name. *Shit!* My mind raced, searching for a believable one, a believable Thai nickname. The only one I could think of came from the nametag of the woman who had sold me coffee earlier in the day. "My name is Toon."

"Toon?" He raised his eyebrows.

I only smiled and repeated the name.

"I haven't heard that one before."

I said nothing and continued to smile.

"You speak English?" His line of questioning continued.

"Yes. What's your name?"

The man relaxed his posture and crossed a leg over his lap. "My name is John."

John? I guess we both want to keep our identities a

secret. I turned my body toward him a bit. I wanted a better look at my suitor. He wore black pants and a crisp, white button-down tucked in at the waist. He also had a large silver watch on his left wrist. He stood out from the other customers, mainly because he wasn't interested in the women on stage. He hadn't once glanced at them since taking a seat.

"You don't like what you see?" I asked, motioning with my head.

"I do, but what I see here is much more interesting," he said, quickly looking me over.

He was charming. I gave him that. Not once did he shift his eyes off me for a glance around the room. He could easily make a woman feel as if she were the only one that existed. But I knew better.

Not wanting to mislead the mama-san into thinking I wasn't with Kang, I kept my actions sterile. Kang and I had thought about approaching her and explaining who we were and what we wanted to do, but it seemed like that would bring on more trouble than it was worth. It might have been a different story if Artie had arranged it, but he was busy chasing down the other lead.

My uninterested act didn't work too well. Within seconds, he had placed his hand on my thigh and given it a gentle squeeze. *He better not slide that hand higher.*

He had moved closer, and I could smell his cologne. It had a light, woodsy scent. Not overpowering, just enough to be pleasant. I glanced at his hands; his nails were neatly manicured and his palms were smooth—an office worker? His shirt was soft, a quality blend of cotton. He wore silver cufflinks in the shape of a "C." *Is that a designer or a personal design?*

"Do you work here?" he asked.

"I don't dance."

"I can see that." He looked at my glass. "Can I buy you a drink?"

Where the hell is Kyle? "Yes. I'm drinking Jameson, neat."

He signaled for the service attendant and ordered our drinks. I took that opportunity to give the room another once-over. I still didn't see a man that fit our description. I looked at my watch again. A half hour had passed. Surely it didn't take that long for Kang to survey the second level, unless there were more. Not wanting to blow my cover, I continued my conversation with the man who called himself John. *The irony.*

Throughout our small talk, I faked the sips of my cocktail to keep my head level. He didn't seem to notice that my drink wasn't disappearing. I continued to smile as he talked about his job and why he was in Bangkok. I suddenly felt like I was beginning to understand what these women had to endure on a nightly basis. I'm sure every man and every conversation blurred. While I wasn't terribly bored, I found myself only half listening to him. I was more concerned about keeping an eye on the men entering the establishment.

After another fifteen minutes had passed, my patience started to wane. At that point, I had to give these women credit. I don't know how they feigned interest all night, every night. I almost rolled my eyes when he started to tell me that he was the head regional sales rep for blah, blah, blah and how he got an award for blah, blah, blah. Getting paid to have sex might seem easy, but what I learned that night was that there was a whole lot of mind-numbing work leading up to that payday. *This conversation reminds me of a few dates I've had.*

As much as I wanted to find out what Kang was up to, I knew I needed to keep an eye on the entrance. Plus, I had John providing the perfect cover. But as my luck would have it, the dynamics changed when he slid his hand farther up my thigh and asked, "Want to come back to my hotel room?"

Chapter 43

The Creeper stood and moved across the room, away from the woman whose thigh he'd had the pleasure of groping recently. He took a seat on the upper level and barked his drink order to the server who was upon him in seconds. His charming smile had been replaced by a scowl worthy of Scrooge.

The Creeper had never had his advances rejected, at least not from a woman at a bar. But he supposed she had good reason; she already had a customer, who had returned just as the Creeper's hand had met her lacy underwear. Not wanting to create a scene, he had taken the high road and bowed out of the situation as quickly as he had entered it.

There he sat, alone, with his grip on the beer bottle tighter than usual. An assembly line of expletives rolled off his tongue but fell upon deaf ears thanks to the large speaker mounted to the wall above his head. He continued to stare at the woman and her date. They were so stupid to think he would give up easily.

She's my date. She's my date, the Creeper mouthed. He didn't care that she was someone else's date; nobody decided who he could and couldn't have. *How dare they disrespect me?* He had killed many for less. He wanted to kill them. But he knew recklessness was his enemy. It took all the strength he had to not to rush across the room and slam his beer bottle over their heads.

The Creeper reached into his pants pocket and removed his cell phone. He opened the browser and navigated to the Chasing Chinatown game. His curiosity of the next task had gotten the better of him the other day, even though a week ago he had sworn off playing the game.

Funny how things work out, he thought as he watched the animated scroll unravel and reveal two pictures: one of Agent Abby Kane and one of Detective Kyle Kang. While intrigued at the time, he hadn't yet decided whether or not to pursue this task—until that night. He assumed all of the luck in the world had to have been working in his favor for him to meet the petite agent purely by chance. It had rendered a decision for him.

The Creeper looked up from his phone and focused on the transparent couple huddled across the room. His smile had returned.

Chapter 44

"Sheesh, I walk away for a minute and you're already out on the prowl looking for some other guy," Kang said.

I chuckled at his joke. "Excuse me, but you were gone for more than a minute. Were there other floors?"

"Nah, but I got cornered by the mama-san and two of her girls. I had to buy them a drink to get out of there."

"Yeah, I'm sure you were faced with the same impossible escape that the inmates at Alcatraz were up against."

Kang brushed me off and looked across the room toward the blond man who had recently occupied the seat next to me. "So who's the guy?"

"John."

"Yeah, I know he's a john, but what's his deal?"

"Actually, he said his name was John. He's here for the same reason every other man is, except he was interested in me and not the dancers."

Kang pulled his head back. "He just plopped himself down? You didn't invite him?"

"Are you crazy? I know I'm undercover, but I'm not actively soliciting men."

Kang muttered something before looking back across the room.

"Someone sounds jealous," I sing-songed.

"Puh-lease. I have a girlfriend."

"Oh, so I guess when you got leg-locked by that ladyboy our first night in town, that didn't count as straying."

"What? I was being nice. And I didn't know she...he...was a ladyboy."

"I'd like to hear you explain that one to Sushi."

"It's *Suzi*. And why don't you like her?"

"I like her," I lied as I struggled to keep a straight face. Kang crinkled his brow. "No you don't. I can tell."

"What?" I continued, my eyes shot open and my mouth fell agape as I tried to conjure total innocence.

"I know you don't like her. It's so obvious that *you're* the one *who's* jealous."

Oh, tell me he did not just go there. "Look, just because you're attached to some*thing* and I'm single doesn't mean I'm jealous. By the way, unless you're blind, she's the one who doesn't like me."

We both picked up our glasses to give each other the impression that we were too busy drinking to speak. At least, that was the reason why I took a thousand mini-sips in a row without removing my cup from my lips. But there was a bigger question: Why on earth *was* I feeling jealous? I thought for sure I had shaken off the crush I had developed on him when we had been in the hospital together. Had I only fooled myself into believing that? Did I actually like Kang, and had I only realized it when he suddenly wasn't available?

"You're right," he said.

"About what?"

"Suzi's a bit jealous of our relationship. I keep telling her that it's strictly professional—"

"Of course it is. Nothing happening here." I pointed between the two of us.

"It's probably the reason why she hasn't warmed up to you entirely."

Warmed up? You mean the Ice Queen is capable of that?

"Don't worry about it though. Things aren't so great between us right now."

Yippee! "Why?"

"Eh, it's the same reason why we broke up in the first place. She can, at times, be a little bitchy."

"A little?" I blurted. *Wait. Did I actually just say that out loud?*

Kang shot me a look.

"I mean, what do you mean by a little?"

"You know. She nags."

"Oh, yeah. I heard men don't like that."

"I'm serious. She critiques every single thing I do. She's such a perfectionist. Nothing I do is right. Yet she relies on me to do everything for her."

"Why are you with her if she is such a *nagger*?" I emphasized with air quotes.

Kang shrugged and took another sip of his beer.

"You need to find a woman who appreciates you for who you are, someone beautiful but who is also independent and capable of doing for herself."

"What, you mean someone like you?"

"Yes, *like* me but not *actually* me." *But it could be me.*

Chapter 45

A crushing blow to his left cheek sent the handcuffed man flying from the chair to the wet floor of the small room. The left side of his face had swelled like a puffer fish, and his eye had disappeared between two folds of fatty skin.

Two men picked him up off the floor and sat him back in the chair. A second later, another blow to the face sent him right back to where he had just lain. That time, there was an audible pop on impact. His cheekbone had finally taken all it could and shattered. Again, the same two men picked him up and placed him back on the chair.

Before the puncher could wind up and deliver another punishing blow, the door to the room opened, and in walked Artie.

The three men, all members of the Royal Thai Police, turned to the detective. The one who had delivered the beating picked up a cloth and wiped his bloody fist clean. Artie moved closer until he stood in front of the seated man. He placed a hand on the man's chin and tilted his face upward so he could look him in his one good eye.

"Having fun?" Artie asked, his tone expressionless.

The man, known on the street as Chan, said nothing.

"My men are not tired. They love this part of the job."

Chan still said nothing.

Artie let go of his face and asked his men if he had said anything.

Bo, the one who lent his fist to the interrogation process, spoke up. "Nothing yet, but the night is young."

Artie didn't have all night. He needed answers now. He looked around the bare storage room. There were a few half-filled paint cans against the wall next to a table. But on the floor in the corner, Artie saw something of interest: a hammer.

He picked it up off the floor and asked one of his men to place a table in front of the seated man.

This got Chan's attention. "What do you want?"

"What do we want? I think you know why we are here."

The man shook his head and looked down. A strand of red-stained saliva stretched from the corner of his mouth and rested on his pant leg. Artie motioned for two of his men to hold Chan in place while he instructed the other to hold his right hand still.

Artie rested the flattened metal head on the knuckle bridge of Chan's hand. "Maybe this will remind you." He took a deep breath as he raised the hammer high above his head before bringing it down with all the force he could muster.

The hammer slammed into Chan's fingers, shattering

bone and splitting one along the left side. A splatter of blood shot up.

Artie didn't stop there. He continued to hammer at the man's hand as fast and as hard has he could.

A loud cry erupted from Chan's open mouth. He screamed for them to stop as he struggled to escape.

But Artie continued to hammer away as if he were tenderizing a piece of raw meat. He was.

Only when Chan's hand no longer resembled its original shape did Artie stop. Blood had pooled under the mound of flesh. Off to the side, a fingernail lay unattached. Chan wept, his mouth frozen open as he looked at the bloody mess at the end of his wrist.

Artie's man released Chan's right hand but quickly grabbed his left and held it against the table. Artie rested the hammer once again on the knuckles.

"No! No!" Chan cried out.

Artie raised the hammer high above his head.

"Somchai ordered us to attack the FBI agent and the detective. Please, I speak the truth."

Artie had heard of that man, Somchai, but had not had the pleasure of actually meeting him.

"Where can we find him?"

"Chinatown... the building behind the T&L Seafood Restaurant... fifth floor."

"Are there men stationed outside?"

"Yes, two at the entrance of the building and two more

on each floor."

"And the room, how many are in there?"

Chan took a moment to think. "Maybe three or four, not including Somchai. Please," he continued, "you must believe me. I'm telling you the truth."

Artie gave the man a comforting smile. "This is good. I appreciate your cooperation." But since he had already raised the tool high above his head, he brought it hammering down one last time.

Chapter 46

Artie was well aware of the political dance that the Thai government had with the men who ran Chinatown. It frustrated him to no end that the neighborhood governed itself how it saw fit. Every police officer in Bangkok knew to tread lightly when it came to policing the area. Sure they had a presence in the area, but presence was all they had. Aside from the police issuing tickets for minor infractions, the residents were left to handle their own affairs.

Infiltrating Chinatown wasn't something Artie took lightly. He had a lot to consider, and he needed to think hard about whether it was worth it. On one hand, all the information he had amassed to date pointed to Somchai as the man who ran the Chasing Chinatown game. On the other hand, the evidence that formed this conclusion was circumstantial.

There was another dilemma: He would be acting without Kane and Kang. He didn't feel the need to bring them into the conversation, even though dismantling the game was their objective and his was to capture the serial killer running loose in his city. Officially, they were here to consult. Artie had already given the two more leeway than he should have. If he wanted, he could take it all back.

Artie also knew that if he took down the mastermind behind the game, he would receive recognition and silence Tip's constant nagging that he didn't do enough to further his career. The Americans would have to trust that he was acting in everyone's best interest and settle for partial credit. Or none.

Artie looked at Chan. A bullet to the back of the head had him slumped on the floor. He watched as his men rolled the lifeless body onto an old tarp they had spread out next to him. This wasn't the first time someone had "gone missing" under Artie's watch. But to his defense, it only happened to degenerates, those who didn't deserve to live.

Once he'd had the body removed and the room cleaned, Artie sent word to a group of his most trusted and highly trained officers to meet him immediately at the Thai restaurant in the Sathorn district just off of the Rama IV highway. He knew the owner and was allowed access to a backroom the restaurant used occasionally for large parties, but Artie used the space periodically for meetings that he preferred no one but the attendees be aware of.

Artie had to act fast on information he had recently obtained. He figured he had three days at the most before Chan was noticeably missed. With the element of surprise on his side, Artie intended to take full advantage of it.

Politics aside, the other great danger would be the resistance at the targets' location. According to Chan, Artie and his men would have to bypass at least fourteen guards who were most likely armed and had some degree of tactical training. Of course Artie had never expected to waltz in and handcuff Somchai without resistance, but he certainly hadn't thought he would encounter that many men.

Even if he could apprehend Somchai alive, leaving Chinatown could prove to be just as problematic. The residents might be alerted and become very protective of the man who kept order. Lastly, he had no plans to inform his superiors of the assault. If wrong, the political fallout would surely cost Artie his job with the Royal Thai Police. Artie would have to prove beyond all doubt that Somchai was indeed the man behind a game designed to kill innocent Thais. That would be enough to forgive his insubordination.

Later that night, five men, including Artie, gathered at a round table filled with platters of spicy curries, steamed fish, and wok-fried vegetables. His men wasted no time digging into the dishes. Artie allowed them time to get at least one plate of food down their throats before clearing his.

"You all know why you're here." Artie looked each man directly in the eyes before continuing. "As always, the mission is dangerous. You could get hurt. You could die. If you survive either of those realities, know that, this time, you also face the risk of losing your job. If you don't like what I've just said, then you can leave now."

The room remained quiet as the men eyed each other, waiting to see if someone would step back. No one did. Ever.

"Who's the target?" asked Koi, a bald man with a prominent scar across his chin. He was one of Artie's most trusted collaborators.

"Somchai Neelapaijit, the man in charge of Chinatown."

The men responded to Artie's answer by swallowing hard, shifting in their chairs or both.

Koi spoke up again. "You understand what you're asking of all us?" He motioned around the table with his hand.

"I do, and my offer to leave still stands."

No one moved.

"I take that to mean you're all in."

The men remained quiet as Artie briefed them on the Chasing Chinatown game and Somchai's connection to it. When he concluded, they remained silent.

"Any questions?" Artie asked after a brief pause.

"One," Koi said, breaking the silence. He met eyes with the other men before continuing. "Are we taking him alive?"

Artie grinned. "We take him any way we can."

Chapter 47

It was after midnight. Kang and I both had realized we needed help from Artie and his department to track down Team Creeper. We had wanted to avoid, or at least minimize, involving the police, since we weren't officially here to investigate, and we didn't want anything to be misconstrued.

But at this point, we needed to be able to conduct surveillance on the premises or near the bar without being bothered by the mama-sans or the dancers. Our hope was that Artie could arrange this without word leaking of our presence. I was doubtful but remained positive.

We also needed other teams positioned along the soi so they might help us keep an eye out for this guy. The way we saw it, there was no other way to avoid a needle-in-a-haystack situation.

I put a call in to Artie but got his voicemail. I left a brief message explaining our situation and asking for a meeting. After I hung up, Kang and I called it a night and headed out of the bar. Before exiting, I looked to where the interested blond man had taken a seat and saw that it was empty. My guess was that he had found another toy to play with.

The walk back to the hotel was uneventful. I couldn't wait to ditch the dress and shoes and throw on my comfy sweatpants. Kang wanted a quick snack before heading up to our room, but I didn't have it in me to saddle up at a nearby noodle cart. I know; unbelievable, right? But I was drained.

After parting with Kang, I walked through the lobby and rounded the corner to find nobody standing near the bank of elevators, which thrilled me, of course. A straight shot up to my floor.

Of course, what was I thinking? Here came the downpour on my happy parade.

Right before the elevator door shut, a hand slipped through and bounced the doors back open. I thought Kang had changed his mind about eating. I was wrong and surprised. Standing before me was the blond gentleman from the bar.

"Oh, hello," he said, pausing a beat before entering the lift. "You're not following me are you?"

"I almost said the same thing."

"What happened to your date?" He re-pressed the floor button I had already pressed.

"He's in the room waiting for me. You're still out of luck."

"So it seems. So it seems." He smiled and let his eyes settle on the digital numbers that counted the floors.

When the elevator stopped and the doors opened, he held his hand out, motioning me to exit first. "I hope you enjoy your night."

I smiled but said nothing as I walked by him. I turned left and, from the sound of it, knew he had turned right. I was relieved that his room was in the opposite direction. After a few steps, I looked back, because the coincidence was too much for me. That's when my phone rang. I saw that it was Po Po's cell and answered right away.

"Hi, Mommy!"

Lucy had recently learned how to dial me from Po Po's "favorites" list and had taken to sneaking the phone from her and calling me.

"Hi, sweetie. How are you?"

"I'm oookayyy."

It was early Saturday morning in San Francisco, no school. My guess was that she was up for the cartoons, but I didn't hear the TV in the background, which was a good thing. The TV rule: Thirty minutes in the morning, afternoon, and evening. Harsh? Probably. I felt her time was better spent drawing, reading, singing, playing dress-up, or whatever. So long as she wasn't stagnant in front of the television, it made me happy.

"Does Po Po know you have her phone?"

"Noooooo. I'm hiding." Lucy giggled.

I couldn't help but laugh myself. I had just opened the door to my room when a sharp pain exploded in my back, and I flew forward.

Chapter 48

"Mommy?"

Lucy's call for her mother went unanswered as she heard a scream on the other end of the line.

"Mommy," her voice quivered, "are you okay?"

Still no response, but Lucy could clearly hear a commotion and her mother's voice, strained and then muffled.

Lucy may have been only six, but she was old enough to realize that something was wrong. Again she called out for her mom but heard no response.

Tears welled and streamed down both of her cheeks as she cried out, "Mommy!" over and over, with each call louder than the last until she was screaming uncontrollably into the phone. Her breaths turned to short gasps. Unmentionable images filled her head. Her body shivered, and her teeth chattered.

Over and over, she shouted into the phone, her mouth the only body part that seemed to work. The rest of her tiny frame remained frozen in the dark closet, where she often had gone to call her mother.

Ryan heard Lucy first and shot off his bed. "Lucy!" he

called out as he sprinted toward her room. There was no response, only the same wailing cry for their mother.

He turned the corner and faced an empty room. "Lucy!" he called once again before moving toward her closet and sliding the door open. Inside, he saw his sister huddled into a tiny ball, shaking uncontrollably with her eyes looking past him. She had Po Po's cell phone pressed tightly against her ear as she pleaded over and over for their mother to answer.

Ryan pried the cell phone from Lucy's hand and put it up to his ear.

"Abby!" he shouted. It was worse than he had expected. He could hear loud crashing noises on the other end. *A fight!* "Abby!" he called out once again. "Are you okay? What's happening?"

For the first time in his life, Ryan felt a sense of hopelessness as he listened to the sound of glass breaking and yet another curdling scream from his mother.

All the judo classes, all the boxing sessions, all the advice she had ever given him over the years had at that moment been rendered completely useless.

The loud crashing noises were soon laced with the sound of smacking that could only be caused by a balled-up fist. Tears formed in his eyes as he told himself over and over that she was tough, that what he heard was her delivering those punishing blows, that she was in control and winning the battle. It had to be. The other outcome was unthinkable for him.

And yet, that very thought had gone ahead and wormed its way into his head. Vivid imagery of her being thrown around a room like a rag doll came to life. Grunts and cries of pain only reinforced his imagination. It was enough to break Ryan's dam of strength. And as much as he tried to prevent that from happening for Lucy's sake, he couldn't. Down his face ran streams of hopelessness, inciting more fear in his sister.

Ryan choked as he tried to call out once again, unable to form even the simplest of sentences. A mumbled mess was all he could muster. And it would only get worse when he heard her yell the one word he had never heard his mother ever utter:

"Help!"

Chapter 49

My attacker and I struggled over a broken glass vase, the jagged edge only inches away from plunging into my neck. He was stronger, and I wasn't sure how much longer I could fend him off. I had myself convinced I needed a miracle.

But Kang would do.

"Drop it!" I heard him shout.

The blond man stole a look over his shoulder and gave me the small window of opportunity I needed to save my butt. He let up on his downward pressure and I was able to twist his hand around, shoving the shard upward and ripping his left cheek open. He yelled and let go of the weapon we had been fighting over. Without thought, I drove it into his neck—again and again.

He tried to defend my attack with his forearms, but the glass continued to find its mark on any part of his body. A second later, Kang yanked him off of me and pinned him to the ground, ready to continue the fight, but it became clear to us both that the fight was already over.

His heart pumped warm blood out of the wounds in his neck and arms. I got to my feet and reached for the hotel phone, hitting the button for the front desk. "I need the police and an ambulance immediately. A man is dying."

My attacker lay on his side, barely moving. Kang used both hands to apply pressure to the largest wound on his neck. I grabbed hold of Kang's weapon and kept it trained on the man.

Blood was smeared across his face, and more of it seemed to seep through Kang's fingers. I hurried to the bathroom and returned with a hand towel. It would do a better job at stopping the blood flow. While it was only seconds ago that this man had wanted me dead, we both knew it was important to keep him alive.

"Why did you try to kill me?" I shouted. "Was this because of what happened at the club?"

His eyes found me. A weak smile appeared on his face. I swear; if it hadn't been for the damage I had caused to his neck, he would have laughed.

I searched his pockets and found his wallet and passport. Both pieces of identification shared the same information: John Royker from Johannesburg, South Africa. The location matched his accent.

"You followed us here from the club. Why?" I continued my questioning.

Still, he said nothing and only smiled. He was dying. There was no denying that. But all I cared about was extracting as much information from him as possible before the inevitable took place.

"You think it's funny to kill people?" No sooner had those words left my lips than an idea of who this man might be took over my thoughts. *Could it be? But our guy has dark hair and a limp.* And yet, as I flashed back over the night's events, it was clear to me that he had targeted me; he'd had no interest in any other woman in that club.

Was he the Creeper? Did he work alone? As I stared into his eyes, his pupils were enlarged and jittery, yet he seemed to be experiencing great joy in what had just taken place. A psychopath enjoying the spotlight, even in his darkest hour.

"You're Team Creeper!"

He gurgled a faint laugh before closing his eyes.

Kang shook the man in an effort to keep him awake. I asked the same question, wanting a definite answer to my hypothetical guess. He faded in and out of consciousness for few more seconds before taking his last breath and leaving me without a reply.

When hotel security arrived at our room seconds later, there was a motionless body on the carpeted floor, and Kang and I were covered in blood. Add that I held a weapon in my hand, and I could understand how incriminating it looked—for us.

The next few minutes were extremely tense as we worked to defuse the situation and explain what had happened. Fortunately, we both had identification on us. It was the turning point in the shouting match between us and the trio of suited security guards, *and* it was the only reason for them to believe us.

The police and paramedics arrived shortly after. Our guy was long gone and needed a body bag. We, however, had the arduous process of having to explain what had happened again and again to every officer who arrived on the scene. While our identification kept us out of handcuffs, the language barrier continued to thwart our efforts for a speedy explanation. Each person wanted to hear it from our mouths and not from those who had already received the details. It was Thai bureaucracy at its worse.

Artie surprised us by arriving a half hour after the police had. "Abby. Kyle. What the hell happened here?" His eyes fluttered between us and the body lying next to the bed.

"How did you know we were here?" I questioned his question.

"Word about an FBI agent involved in a murder got back to one of my men, and he contacted me. I tried calling your cell, but I got no answer."

"My phone!" I only then just remembered that I had been talking with Lucy when I was attacked. I scanned the dark brown carpeting for my phone, wondering if she had heard any of what had taken place. I hoped she hadn't.

I found my cell near the wall. The line was dead. I tried calling Po Po but instead heard a recording that told me my phone was out of money. *Great.* I picked up the hotel phone and dialed home.

Chapter 50

Po Po picked up on the first ring. That told me she had been eagerly waiting for a call.

"Abby!"

"Yes, it's me."

"You okay. What happened? Lucy was crying."

"I'm fine. Where's Lucy?"

"Sleeping. She was so upset earlier. What happened?"

I came clean with my mother-in-law. She needed to know what had happened. She would be the one having to deal with the immediate fallout back home. "Long story short, I was attacked while I was talking to Lucy. I lost my phone in the scuffle, and she must have heard the commotion," I said, softening the night's events. If Lucy had heard everything, well, there was no sense in rehashing it and upsetting Po Po as well.

Po Po told me Ryan had found Lucy tucked away in her closet, holding the phone to her ear and sobbing.

"Wait. Ryan found her?" This thought had never entered my mind. Now I had to worry about what he had heard.

"Abby, Ryan told me what he hear on the phone. You

not have a small fight. He cry, too, you know. He said you were being hurt. He hear you call for help."

A wave of emotions erupted in my chest and raced throughout my body. I felt my legs grow weak, and my stomach did back flips. My breaths grew short as my mind put on a slideshow of the imagery that my kids might have dreamt up.

I had officially become the worst mother on planet Earth.

I had inadvertently put my kids through an unimaginable situation, one no mother would ever want their children to experience. Who in their right mind would subject their kids to that psychological damage? *Me, the selfish crime-fighter.* I had made my own children believe that their mother, their protector, the one person who they could always count on to provide them with comfort and love and be their happy place had been killed.

The hotel phone was cordless, so I moved my conversation into the bathroom and locked the door. Next came the tears. I tried to hold them back. No way could I be the one who loses it. The backbone of a family doesn't do that. I'm the rock. I'm the one the others can turn to—the solution to a problem. And yet, I had done the opposite and hurt the ones I loved the most.

Po Po told me that, when she had gotten to Lucy's room, she'd found both children wailing uncontrollably. She said Ryan had been holding her cell phone, but the line was dead when she had checked it.

"I redial the last number, but I only get a Thai recording, and I don't understand."

"Rotten timing. My phone ran out of time right about then."

"When I ask Ryan what happened, he only able to tell me bits and pieces but enough to know something bad happen on phone."

Listening to Po Po fill in the blanks devastated me. Every word from her mouth was a slug to my gut. I doubled over with guilt and struggled for breaths. At that moment, I felt like a complete failure. I didn't deserve the three of them.

Both children were asleep, and I asked Po Po not to wake them. I told her I would talk to them later, but she ignored me and had already made her way to Ryan's room.

Before I could get another word out, I heard his voice.

"Abby, you're okay," he said, sniffling.

"Yes, sweetie. I'm fine. I'm all right."

"I was so worried. I heard a fight, and I heard you screaming, and you needed help, and—"

"Shhhh. Everything is fine. Your mom is okay. You hear me? I'm okay."

"I thought you had... you were—"

"What? What did you think? You know better. I'm your tough mom."

He sniffed and coughed. "Yeah, I do. You're my tough

mom."

"That's right. I'm your tough mom, and nothing is ever going to happen to me. I want you to understand that."

"Okay," He sniffed. I heard rustling on the phone and then the sweet sound of my youngest.

"Mommmyyy!" Lucy shouted in the phone. "I was so worried about you. You sounded like you were in trouble."

"Mommy is okay. I'm not hurt. Mommy had a little problem, but it's all over now. Everything is fine, and I'll be home soon."

Lucy continued to cry and tell me that she missed me. After a few seconds, Po Po came back on the line.

"Ryan take Lucy back to her room. Better for her to rest."

I didn't know what to say. My son had just left to console his sister, my daughter. That was my job—another blatant sign that I had, once again, failed as a parent. Wait. Forget that. I had failed at being a good person, period. *What the hell is wrong with me?*

After a few seconds of silence, Po Po asked when I was coming home. I didn't have an answer and said what I always said. "Soon."

There was a knock on the door followed by Kang's voice. "Abby, is everything okay?"

"Yeah, I'll be out soon. Just give me a minute." I plucked a few pieces of tissue from a plastic container on the sink counter and dabbed my eyes dry. My left cheek had swelled from a punch I had taken earlier.

"Kyle," I called out.

"Yeah, what is it?"

"Could you get me some ice?"

"I'm on it."

To tide me over, I ran the corner of a hand towel under the faucet and pressed it against my face. It felt cool against the warm throbbing that had become much more noticeable now that my adrenaline rush had dissipated.

I looked myself over in the mirror, cleared my throat, shook off my emotions, and put on my best face. A beat later, I exited the bathroom, ready for business.

Chapter 51

A paramedic approached me and handed me an ice pack. Kang and Artie were right behind him. I wrapped the cold compress in the towel and pressed it against my face.

The hotel room was teeming with Thai law enforcement. The body hadn't been moved, and the CSI team was in the early stages of their investigation.

"Abby," Artie said in a low voice, "let us step outside and talk."

Kang and I followed him into the hallway. I knew both of them had the same burning question on their mind. As soon as we were a few feet from the door, I told them what had happened from the moment I had parted ways with Kang outside the hotel.

"You sure this is the same guy from the bar?" Artie asked.

"Positive."

"Abby's right. I remember that guy," Kang added. "He must have been waiting for us outside, because I also remember looking over to where he had been sitting before we left, and I didn't see him."

"His wallet contained a card key belonging to the

Westin hotel," Artie said. "My guys are on their way over there to track down his room. Hopefully they find something that can shed some light on your theory that the body inside that room belongs to the Creeper."

"This is what my gut is telling me," I said. "I don't have any definitive proof except the look in his eyes when he attacked me. It was like he knew who I was. And I don't mean in an I-just-met-you sort of way. It all felt very premeditated. Did you find anything else on his person?"

"A cell phone," Artie responded.

"Did you check to see if the game app is loaded on it?"

The look on Artie's face told me his answer. "Wait here," he said before turning around and heading back into the room. A few seconds later, he reappeared with a smartphone in a baggie. He snapped a glove onto his hand and removed the phone. "We're in luck; no passcode." He continued tapping at the screen until a smile formed on his face. That's when he turned the phone around and showed us the Chasing Chinatown game.

This was the second account within the game that we had access to. From what we could tell, the game play was exactly the same as what we experienced while playing as the Carlsons, except for one detail: The Creeper's second task in Bangkok revealed a picture of Kang and me with the blunt instructions to eliminate us.

"So your masked man told the truth," Kang said as he rested his hands on his hips.

"Yep, and they got what they wanted: a dead creep," I said, folding my arms across my chest.

"So now what?" Artie asked. "We won the battle. Does that mean we can keep playing the game?"

Neither Kang nor I had an answer for him. My best guess was that, once word got back to the mastermind that the Creeper had become a stiff, the accounts for Team Carlson and Team Creeper would be shut down.

"Up until now, any progress we've made has come from playing the game, but sadly, I don't think we've gotten closer to the mastermind. We've taken down two teams, yet what I see here on the phone is that the remaining teams are still playing in the other cities."

"Maybe when it becomes apparent that Bangkok has now been compromised, we might see some sort of effect. That body," Kang thumbed backward, "is still warm."

Kang reminded all of us that patience went a long way. Just then, a talk bubble appeared stating that Team Despicable had completed the fourth task in Shanghai, further reinforcing what I had just said.

"I count only seventeen teams," Artie said.

"Rome caught up with the killer in their city," I said. "I got word on that when I spoke to my supervisor a few days ago. Sorry, it slipped my mind. But what I'm trying to say is that this game will continue until a team wins."

"Or all teams are captured," Artie suggested.

"I agree with you there, but taking down the

mastermind is the only way to dismantle the game for good."

"I agree," Kang said. "The way I see it, so long as these dipshits allow us access, we have to keep playing. It's the only card we have."

"Don't forget, Artie: Another team could pass through Bangkok. The only way to take Bangkok off the list of destinations, like we did in San Francisco, is to take out whoever is responsible for managing the game here."

Artie looked around to make sure we were alone. "I think I know who that person is."

Chapter 52

"I'm pretty sure Somchai Neelapaijit is our guy." Artie beamed. His eyebrows arched proudly. He summarized what he had discovered after securing and interrogating the individual who had attacked us.

"Where is this guy?" Kang asked. "I'd like a crack at him."

"Where he is isn't important," Artie said quickly. "We obtained the information we needed, and right now, my men are fleshing out the details of my plan. It's important that we execute it as quietly and as fast as possible."

"Why?" I asked.

"A combination of things. The Triads have a tight grip on the neighborhood, and Chinatown is off limits to Thai police thanks to corrupt politicians."

"It's no different than what we faced back in San Francisco. I suspect every Chinatown, to some degree, is self-governing for the very reasons you just stated," Kang added.

"And you think this is the way to go, under the radar?" I asked. "Going rogue, so to speak?"

"I do. I know it makes the operation ten times more

dangerous, but if we try to play by the rules, we'll be buried in red tape and lose our chance at surprising Somchai. And if for some reason bureaucracy didn't get in the way, someone would tip him off, and he'd go into hiding. I'm sure of that."

I understood what he faced. We were in Thailand. They had a different way of handling things. My thoughts were that it wasn't much of a hurdle for Artie to overcome, but I had to make sure that, if things did go wrong, Kang and I weren't caught up in it, or worse, victimized by it. We had already experienced our fair share of close calls on this trip. Even Reilly had thoughts of pulling me out. Another stumble and I knew we would be kissing our time here goodbye.

"You know," I said, "if you're right about this guy, I think we might have a link."

"What do you mean?" he asked.

"Well, Jing Woo managed the game in San Francisco, and he oversaw the city's Chinatown. If the same holds true for this Somchai guy, then the head Triad in each Chinatown may also be in charge of running the game."

"Hmmmm." Kang removed a handkerchief from his pocket and took the cell from Artie. "Son of a... I don't know why I didn't see the connection before." He turned the phone around to show us the list of cities still in play. "Every single one of these cities features a prominent Chinatown."

"What are you, some sort of authority on Chinatown?" Artie asked.

A grin appeared on my face, and Kang chuckled. "Let's just say it's a hobby of mine."

Artie seemed to be at a loss.

"Kyle here is kind of a nerd about all things Chinese," I explained. "If we're right about this, my supervisor can alert our partners around the world to focus on Chinatowns. If they take out the management, it stops the game play there."

"But it doesn't stop the killer," Artie said, stretching out his arms, palms up.

"No, it doesn't, but it may stop more unnecessary deaths," I said.

We had turned a corner on our investigation and gained ourselves another solid foothold. Would it lead us to the mastermind? I was hopeful. I knew if we continued to squeeze, we would close in on him.

"When do you think your men will be ready?"

"Soon. Look, I don't expect you two to tag along. I understand the implications that you might face should things go wrong, not only with our government but with your superiors as well. I'm willing to take this on by myself."

I looked at the ice pack in my hand and thought about what I had just put my two children through. I thought about why I had moved my family from Hong Kong to San Francisco. I thought about how I wanted a quieter, safer, and much more normal life for us. I thought about how I wasn't nearly delivering on that as well as I could be.

I had already experienced two life-threatening situations and felt extremely lucky with the outcomes. Quite frankly, I wasn't too excited about rolling the dice yet a third time. Not to mention the fact that we would definitely be overstepping what little authority we had here in Thailand. From the look in Kang's eyes, I could see that he had similar thoughts.

This was a quagmire of epic proportions. I didn't want to leave Artie to handle the case by himself. This was *my* investigation.

On the other hand, we could be jeopardizing the solid foothold we had recently gained by *not* following Artie's plan. We were moving fast, cutting corners, and not thinking things through thoroughly. At least that was how I felt.

"I understand that this is a lot to take in," Artie said, breaking the silence and gaining our attention again. "As soon as my men and I have everything in place, I'll brief you two. You can give me your answer then."

Artie had just given us a little breathing room, and I intended to take those much-needed breaths.

Chapter 53

A quick peek at my watch told me it was three in the morning. I was battered and beat. As soon as we were no longer needed at the crime scene, we left. We agreed to grab a few hours of shut-eye before discussing our options and what our approach to the investigation should be from that point on. The situation had changed, and we needed to reevaluate.

Neither of us thought we would be endangering ourselves by returning to our original hotel, the Landmark Plaza. If we were still being watched, checking into yet a third hotel would be pointless. In our minds, we weren't facing a credible threat.

Artie, on the other hand, whether he realized or not, never questioned how we had ended up with a room at the Sheraton, and I didn't feel the need to offer up an explanation that wasn't, at the time, being asked for.

What little of the night that was left sped by fast. That's how it felt when a morning wakeup call from Artie interrupted my Zs. He had called to tell me that they had discovered evidence in the room at the Westin that confirmed what we already thought: The man who attacked me was the Creeper.

"We found a wig and colored contact lenses that match our original description."

"What about the limp everyone kept reporting?"

"We found a metal device in his suitcase that looks like a rudimentary splint. We believe he wore this, and that's what caused him to limp. He played the game under a disguise, Abby."

"If that's the case, I highly doubt we would have ever caught up with him if he hadn't made the first move. Even my kidnappers hadn't known he had changed his appearance."

"Luck was on our side."

"No kidding."

Before I could thank Artie for the update, he surprised me by saying he had a finalized plan in place for capturing Somchai.

"That was fast."

"Time is against us. I'd like to meet with you and Kyle right away to discuss the details and how you two can be involved if need be."

If need be? It sounded like Artie had just laid the groundwork for our participation to be hands-off. I decided to reserve judgment and told him we could meet in one hour at the Starbucks. I then rang Kang and relayed my conversation with Artie.

"Disguise? Sheesh, we got lucky."

"I agree."

"So this sense that Artie might be trying to spearhead the investigation from here on out, is that a bad thing? I mean we *are* in Thailand and don't have any authority. And we've already had more than our fair share of hairy moments. It might be smart to let him take the lead on this operation."

"There's certainly merit in that approach. I don't know how finalized the plan is. Everything we've done up to date has been kind of a shoot-from-the-hip approach, and that's exactly the impression I got when Artie talked about this last night. Plus, he wanted to keep the entire operation hush-hush."

"It's like we're setting ourselves up for more problems by being involved."

"That's what I'm thinking. My brain is telling me to take a step back, but my ego is bruised."

"Hey, we're only two people. Our own investigation is already under the radar. Why put ourselves farther off the grid?"

I couldn't argue with Kang. He was right. We lacked the proper support and equipment we would need to infiltrate Somchai's hideout and extract him successfully. In the end, we decided to hear Artie out before making any decisions. Maybe he did have a credible plan in place.

Chapter 54

When we arrived at the coffee shop, Artie was already inside. He had coffee for Kang and hot water for me. He stood and shook both our hands and, before we could take our seats, started discussing his plan.

"We plan on hitting Somchai at three in the morning. Chinatown will be a sleeping giant at that time."

So far, I nodded in agreement. I removed my tin of loose-leaf tea and dropped a pinch into my hot water. It felt so good to be reunited with the real deal instead of the tea bags I'd been stuck with. *Note to self: Next time, include tea with my emergency change of clothes.*

"Our interrogation revealed that the place is heavily guarded, about fourteen men, and we have to assume they have some degree of tactical training."

"What?" Kang choked on his coffee and followed that up with a small coughing fit.

"What sort of weaponry do they possess?" I said, equally surprised.

"Most will be armed with handguns, but I wouldn't put it past Somchai's men to have a few high-powered rifles in their stock and even be outfitted with flak jackets."

I scratched the top of my forehead. Taking a backseat on this mission was becoming an easy decision.

"There's more. Somchai's office is on the top floor of a five-story building. The men are spread out on every floor. Anything but a silent approach will have bullets raining down upon us."

"Sheesh. What kind of firepower do you have?" Kang asked.

"We have body armor, and we can outgun them with weapons, but a firefight is something we want to avoid. It'll only make the situation worse and our exit out of Chinatown harder. Remember, we have to assume that, if the alarm is sounded, more Somchai supporters will appear."

"Okay, so enlighten us. How do you plan on getting past his men and into his office quietly?" I asked.

"That's the brilliant part of my plan." A grin appeared on Artie's face. "We're not using the front door. The next building sits only three feet away. We can cross over via the roof and enter the top floor from above. We'll leave the same way we came. If all goes as planned, his men won't know a thing."

Finally, a bit of sense amid the madness of his plan. Still, it seemed like the odds were stacked, even if Artie's men were better equipped and trained.

"Is there security at that adjacent building?" I asked.

"I have a contact in that building. He's assured me that

Somchai's men don't have a presence there."

It appeared that Artie had put thought into his plan, but one look at Kang and I knew his thoughts were in line with mine: Let Artie run with this while we watch from the sidelines. But I still wanted to see how much better the plan could get.

"How do you plan on achieving a still, very-much-needed stealthy approach into Chinatown?"

"A delivery truck."

"Okay," I said, "but what about the guards on the top floor? There's no avoiding them."

"That's where you two come in," he said.

Chapter 55

"That's your plan, have us draw the guards out of the building so you can slip in on top unnoticed?" I made no attempt to hide my disappointment, nor did I scale back the sarcasm I delivered with my response. I even threw in an eye roll as I sat back in my seat shaking my head.

"I gotta admit," Kang said, "telling us that our role is to act as the bait isn't a plan. It's a death wish. I want no part of this." Kang pushed back from the table and stood. "Sorry, Abby, but I'm not playing along. I'll be at the hotel if you need me."

I turned to Artie. "Artie, I'm with Kyle on this one. We can't be part of this operation."

"Wait," Artie popped out of his seat with an arm reaching out to me. He motioned for both of us to take out seats again. "At least let me finish explaining."

"Explaining what?" Kang asked. "I'm not offering myself up as bait. So unless that part of your plan changes, I don't see any point in sticking around."

Artie motioned again to the chair.

Clearly that part of the plan wasn't changing, and Kang didn't need to be told that. He turned and walked away.

"Abby?" Artie shrugged while holding his palms up.

"Look, Artie, Kang doesn't work for me. I can't make him do anything. Plus, I agree with him. So long as your plan calls for us to act as the distraction, we're not taking part. It's high-risk, not to mention I would be crossing the line. I have no jurisdiction in Thailand; neither does Kyle. We can't willingly take part in an unsanctioned operation."

Artie leaned over the table. He lowered his voice, but the tone intensified. "What the hell do you call what you're doing now? Technically, you're here to advise, not to investigate. Yet you are. I call the shots, and you report to me, but I decided to work with you rather than treat you how you should have been treated—like a nuisance in my country.

I moved closer and lowered my own voice. "Oh, please. You need my expertise. This case is over your head, and you know it. Consulting never would have captured the Creeper."

"Typical American arrogance. So it's okay for you to bend the rules where you see fit, but not for me? Tell me, why isn't the American Embassy involved? Where is your liaison? I know you have an FBI and a CIA contact over there. Do they even know you're here? You're cutting corners yourself, and you know it."

I looked over my shoulder to ensure that no one had sat down behind us. I then took a seat. So did Artie. "Look, if you must know. They are aware of my presence here, and I do keep them updated on my activities."

"Oh? Lots of help they were when you got yourself kidnapped. Why weren't they notified? Kyle could have easily done that, yet he called me. And what about last night when you almost got yourself killed? Where were they then?"

Artie was right. I had cut corners. My contact at the embassy had received a very sanitized version of my activities here. I had met with him once and kept all other contact to phone calls. As far as he knew, my days were spent advising the Thai Police on an investigation.

The only person who knew of my real activities, besides Kang, was my supervisor, Reilly. Both understood what was at stake. Getting closer to the mastermind meant keeping the number of people involved to a minimum, even if it meant deceiving one of our own. "They are on a need-to-know basis. And I didn't think what happened merited their involvement. You're right. I have cut some corners, but I did not willingly put myself into those situations. And how do you think it would look if my liaison and the embassy were alerted to a missing FBI agent under your watch?"

I had Artie there. He knew that, if the light had been shed on what had actually taken place, he would have taken the hit for being irresponsible. If he wanted to get even more technical, we were guests of Thailand and his responsibility. Being kidnapped under his watch wouldn't have done Artie's career any favors.

"Okay." Artie shrugged, indifferent to the situation. "So we each have our methods for achieving our results. Now what?"

"What do you mean, 'Now what?' Same-same, as the saying goes; I'm not posing as your decoy, and as you can see, Kyle has already checked out."

Artie gave the coffee shop a once-over, his left leg bouncing a steady stream of beats, before settling his eyes back on me. "You have to admit, the part of my plan that involves coming in from the roof has merit."

I nodded.

"So, help me. What would you do?"

Chapter 56

An hour later, and Artie and I had a revised plan. But in order for it to be effective, we needed two things to happen: Kang had to agree to be a part of it, and we needed an extra two days. Artie was reluctant to postpone, worried that our window of opportunity to take down Somchai might close.

"I can keep the Creeper's death out of the media, but who knows how the game tracks their players?" he said. "And Chan, the Triad member, well, let's just say he's gone missing. Eventually, someone will come looking for him. Time is not on our side."

Artie wanted to move in immediately, but it was a suicide mission. Two days to get our new plan in order provided a better opportunity. We would just have to take the chance that everything went our way and that Somchai stayed put.

I told Artie that it would be better if I talked to Kang alone. I knew he would still be emotional over what had taken place earlier that morning, and seeing Artie would only keep his mind shut to other possibilities.

I tracked Kang down outside the hotel. He had just ordered a bowl of noodles, so I joined him. We slurped the white thin strands and spooned porky broth into our mouths for a good ten minutes before I broached the subject of Somchai.

"Are you crazy? You heard what he said."

"That's the old plan. There's a new one," I said, coiling strands of noodles onto a spoon with my chopstick.

"Abby, we're supposed to be here advising—at the most, collecting information—but instead, we're spearheading an investigation without the proper backing and support of our superiors. I could lose my job over this, even my head—literally."

"We talked about this. I thought you were okay with our approach on this case when we got here."

"That was before I got in a street fight and had to pretend to be Evel Knievel to escape an angry mob. And you, Abby, you almost got killed last night. This is beyond tweaking the rules. When you went missing, do you know how close I came to calling your contacts at the embassy? Do you?"

"That situation... It wasn't ideal. Strike that. It plain sucked. You know I would have supported whatever decision you made."

"I could have been responsible for your death. I... I..."

I placed a hand on Kang's shoulder and gave it a gentle squeeze. "You're a good detective and an even better friend."

Kang shook his head slowly as he peered into his bowl.

"We can't take any unnecessary risks."

"I agree."

We both took a moment to reflect on our situation before we picked up our bowls, tilted them back toward our mouth and gulped down the rest of our soup.

I removed a tissue from my purse to wipe my mouth while Kang settled for the back of his hand.

Setting down his bowl, he let out a breath and looked at me. "So what's the plan?"

Chapter 57

Over the next two days, Kang and I worked to solidify the details of the new plan. It still called for Artie to enter the building from the roof and extract Somchai via the same route. Until then, all he had to do was keep eyes on Somchai and be sure he was still in that building when we came for him.

Our first task at hand was to ID the person keeping tabs on Kang and me. With all that had happened to us, it was obvious that we were being watched. With a little counter-surveillance, it didn't take long.

Right away I spotted the girl who had provided us with our answers to the two riddles we had solved earlier. It took a little longer to spot the second person—another girl we had never seen before. My gut told me there could be two, and it had been right. The girls were amateurs in the game of surveillance, but it was essential they never lost sight of us. From that moment on, we made it easier for them to watch and follow us. It was part of the plan.

Secondly, we booked rooms at a new hotel and moved some of our stuff over there to give the impression that we were setting up another safe location. Our tailers were right behind us the entire time, as we expected them to be. It was part of the plan.

Third, with the help of Artie, we met with the owner of the Shark bar in broad daylight. We used a lot of exaggerated hand movements and pointed to various rooftop locations, giving the impression that we were setting up for something at Soi Cowboy. I spotted one of the girls on her cell phone. I was pretty sure she was giving a play-by-play to her boss of what we were doing, which we expected. It was part of the plan.

We then repeated the entire show at Nana Plaza with another bar owner who was friendly with Artie and whom he could trust. We did this once more outside the location of our new hotel. The girls stuck with us the entire time.

Lastly, we hired a tuk-tuk, one of those three-wheel rickshaws, to drive us up and down Sukhumvit Road. Except this time, Artie had his men in two other tuk-tuks following us. Artie pretended to point out various tactical points of interest while talking to his men via two-way radios. Anyone in his or her right mind would easily have concluded that it looked as if we were setting up for a large surveillance operation.

With that part of the plan taken care of, we spent the second of our two days positioning a few men on the rooftops above Nana Plaza, Soi Cowboy, and our new hotel. They were instructed to continually take photographs and to videotape the surrounding area.

As we had hoped, the two girls continued to report our actions, which resulted in additional bodies. Backup had appeared. According to Artie, they were all members of the local Triad gang. That told us one thing: We had grabbed Somchai's attention, and he wanted to know what the hell was happening.

Artie then had a few police officers, outfitted with tactical gear and high-powered rifles, join the other men on the rooftops. Because his men were split up over a half-mile stretch of road, the seven tailers watching our every move split up so they could better keep an eye on Artie's men. And of course, that was part of the plan.

With our dummy surveillance plan up and operational, the three of us headed back to the Landmark, free of any reporting eyes. We then snuck out a back door and into a delivery van that awaited us. Inside were two members of Artie's trusted team.

"Where are we heading to?" Kang asked.

"A restaurant that I use to hold meetings," Artie replied.

Once there, we spent the rest of our time familiarizing ourselves with our roles to ensure that our plan was executed flawlessly. We were still on for that night. It was important that everyone knew what was expected of them. I also did my best to recreate a layout of the building based on my last visit, when I had been kidnapped. "I know it's not exact," I said while placing my drawing down on the table. "I could be wrong, but it'll have to do."

"It's helpful," Artie said, "but I still don't understand why we"—he pointed at himself and motioned to his men— "aren't privy to the other part of your plan."

Clearly keeping our mouths shut on that one detail had been a sticking point for Artie. I didn't blame him. He had shared openly with us while we withheld information, essentially asking him to blindly trust us.

"We've already covered this. In order for Kang and me to participate, we need control over certain aspects of the operation. This is one of them."

"Withholding information? You realize how dangerous this mission is? My men and I are putting our lives on the line."

"I understand that but so far, everything that we had hoped for has happened."

Artie's cell phone rang just then. "Yes, I see… Are you sure?... That's good news."

All eyes in the room were on Artie.

"I just received word that four of Somchai's personal guards have joined the other Triad gang members, most likely to assess the situation," he reported.

"The decoys we planted are working," Kang observed. "This lowers the amount of resistance in the building, which we were hoping for."

"It's better but still dangerous," Artie said. "I still don't know how you two plan on drawing the attention of the guards in front of the building, and hopefully the ones inside, away from their posts."

"We don't plan on doing anything. We've been made. His men know who we are. They'll see us coming a mile away."

Artie threw his arms up out of frustration as his men shifted in their seats and their low rumble of concern grew louder. The tension in the room thickened.

Artie settled his eyes back on me. He bit his lower lip and bounced his legs. He struggled to keep his voice free of anger. "If you don't do anything, then who, Abby? Who will draw the attention of the guards?"

Before I could answer Artie, my phone alerted me to a text message. I stood up, said nothing and walked away from the table.

"Where are you going?" Artie called out after me.

I didn't respond and exited the small banquet room where we had gathered. He started to question Kang for an explanation as I closed the door behind me. A few minutes later, I returned.

I wasn't alone.

Chapter 58

The tall Russian was the first to enter the room, and while I hadn't yet, what I heard painted a pretty good visual of how Artie and his men reacted.

"Who are you?" I heard Artie's elevated voice, followed by the scraping of a chair against the wooden floor.

By the time I had walked through the door, Detective Sokolov had Kang wrapped up in a giant bear hug.

"You sonofabitch. Need me to save your ass again, huh?" he said in his familiar accent.

"Yeah, pipe dreams," Kang answered with a chuckle.

In step behind me was one other person, Agent House. Artie was still on his feet. So were a few of his men. "Artie, it's okay. They're friends, and they're the other part of the plan."

Artie's mouth hung open for a second longer while he worked to rearrange his thoughts into words. "Why didn't you tell me you were bringing help?"

"The giant is Detective Pete Sokolov," I said, addressing the room. "The woman next to me is Agent Tracy House. Both are familiar with the investigation and the sick game fueling it. We're lucky to have them here to help us."

"Abby," Artie started, but I held up a hand, cutting him off.

"I'm sorry. We couldn't risk their identities being compromised. This isn't a trust issue, so don't take it personally. We needed to do this. Can we move on and focus on what we need to do?"

Artie looked at the four of us and then at his men, who were all looking at him. I hoped he would realize we were all on the same team, working together. He nodded and took his seat. His men followed his lead. In a calm voice, he asked me to continue.

"Good." I looked at my watch. "We don't have much time, and it's best spent focusing on our objective."

Artie glanced at his watch. "It's only ten. We're not set to move in until three in the morning, when it's quiet."

"That's what we don't want to do. The remaining guards will be on high alert due to the distraction we created. A quiet and empty street will not be our friend. We need to move in now, while Chinatown is awash with people eating and drinking. We won't be easily detected."

I proceeded to explain that Sokolov and House would pretend to be a couple of inebriated tourists who were lost and seeking directions. "Their goal is to disable the two guards outside the building. It'll reduce the chance of the other guards inside the building being alerted, but it still leaves the guards on the top floor that you will encounter. Because we don't know exactly where the guards are stationed or if they have routine patrols, this prevents us from moving up the floors. It's too risky."

Artie nodded his agreement. "I'm confident we can dispatch the guards on the top floor and gain entrance to Somchai's office. So far, this is a better plan. I'm curious though; what's your role?"

"Kyle and I will operate command central in the delivery van."

"Huh?" Artie's eyebrows crinkled.

"Agent House was able to bring a few toys with her, courtesy of the FBI."

House lifted a black duffle bag onto the table and started unloading equipment.

I picked up a clear earpiece with a wire attached to a small control unit. "Everyone will be equipped with a radio earpiece so that we can all be in contact. There are two throat mics, one for each team. Artie, Agent House can familiarize you with the device."

I then picked up a small, tubular gadget. "We have body-mounted video cameras that can transmit imagery so Kyle and I can monitor the situation in real time. We'll be your eyes. And lastly—this is my favorite part—we have a flexible, fiber-optic video camera."

I picked up the snake-like coil and bent it into a curved shape before handing it to Artie. "You'll be able to slide this under the door and monitor the guards in the hall before entering."

Artie's eyes widened as he snatched the camera from my hand and fiddled with it. His men had already helped themselves to the earpieces and were busy testing them out. "Reilly was a no-go on the video monitor setup you requested," House said. "But this wireless security system we picked up at Best Buy has a portable, nine-inch monitor we can use. I had a tech guy tinker with the system. It can now receive the video feed from the two cameras."

I stretched my lips thin and softened my eyes before giving House a pat to the arm; she always knew how to come through. I spent the next half hour fielding more questions from Artie and his men. With everyone comfortable on the details and their roles in the mission, we gathered our equipment and set out for Chinatown.

Chapter 59

There were two main roads that cut through Chinatown. We would enter the vicinity via the popular Yaorawat Road and exit on Charoen Krung Road. Sokolov and House, Team One, traveled in a taxi ahead of us, while Kang and I plus Team Two, consisting of Artie and his men, followed in the delivery van. We spent that time setting up the video monitor and ensuring our camera feeds, throat mics and earpieces were operational. Our communication system was up and running by the time we reached Chinatown.

Shortly after we passed the ornate arches at the entranceway into the neighborhood, I instructed Team One to exit their taxi and proceed on foot to the target building while we drove ahead to our designated area, the adjacent building.

It took us another twenty minutes to maneuver our vehicle through traffic before parking outside the building. It was located on a street sandwiched between Yaorawat and Charoen Krung, making our escape easy. While small, the side street still had its fair share of street food vendors and sidewalk restaurants, all with tables packed full of patrons. Artie and his men remained in their civilian clothing and carried their tactical gear into the building via duffle bags so as not to draw attention.

The time was 11:45 p.m. and both teams were in position. Kang and I had a live feed from both cameras displayed on our monitor. Team Two had already rendezvoused with Artie's contact. His role was to help them gain entrance to the rooftop and provide the ladder needed to cross the gap between the buildings. I ordered Team Two to proceed to the roof. "Do not cross over to the target building. Hold your position for now."

Team One stood near the lively T&K Seafood restaurant. A very small alley next to it housed the entranceway to Somchai's building.

"Team One, can you get a visual on the guards without entering the alley?"

"That's a negative." House's voice came through clear via her throat mic. "The alley is dark, limiting our visibility."

I couldn't take the chance of Team Two alerting the guards below while they crossed over to the other building. It was imperative that Team One eliminated them beforehand.

I had already brainstormed with House on what the best approach would be for a nonlethal takedown. We wanted to avoid having a body to deal with. The ideal situation called for House and Sokolov to disarm them and tie them up, but we were faced with many unknowns. Were there really only two guards outside? Were there more just inside the doorway? What kind of weapons did they possess? And lastly, how well trained were they in grappling?

I was confident in House and Sokolov's abilities, but as I said, it was not the ideal situation. Another proposition was to use a tranquilizer gun to immobilize them. The problem there was whether or not the guards would be outfitted with body armor.

I knew we would be limited to the sort of gear House could bring with her, and we couldn't plan for a number of scenarios. We had to make our most educated guess and hope for the best. In the end, the drunken, lost tourist guise seemed to play well. It would give House and Sokolov the opportunity to get close so as to assess the guards and the situation.

It would be their call on whether they could disarm and take out the guards. If they felt the situation had become unpredictable, they could pull out without the guards suspecting anything.

Of course, our contingency plan, should that have been necessary, was to remove ourselves from the mission. I made sure Artie understood that. I had received a stern warning from Reilly not to take any unnecessary chances. "If anything goes wrong, Abby, this will come down on you. Is that clear?" Oh, it was very clear.

"Team Two, Team One is still working to assess the situation on the ground."

"Standing by."

"Command, I have an idea," House said. "We could switch our video feed to night vision and maneuver ourselves near the entrance of the alley, perhaps the monitor will show you what we can't see."

"Good idea. Move in."

The video on our monitor turned to a dark green with large patches of white. As Team One moved toward the darkened alley, the heavy light source from the street lamps faded. We picked up a cat crossing their path and a few people walking toward them. House, who wore the video camera, positioned herself so we could look down the dead-end alley. We could hear the two of them giggling and asking each other where they were. They were convincing. Almost too convincing.

"Tracy, I need you to be less drunk; the image is too shaky."

House steadied her movements.

"Pete, I also need you to move to the left of Tracy: you're partially blocking our view."

A beat later, the image opened up, and I could see the figures of two men in the distance. However, there was a problem. "Guys, you won't believe this."

Chapter 60

"What's wrong? What's happening down there?" Artie's voice had popped up in my earpiece. While he and his team were privy to the conversation I'd had with Team One, they didn't have access to a visual.

"Team Two, I need you to continue holding your position until Team One can properly assess the situation."

"Is there a problem?" Artie demanded.

"What do you see?" House chimed in.

"I see two men. One is in a sitting position, leaning back against the building. The other looks to be slumped over next to him. They look like they've passed out."

"That's uncharacteristic of Somchai's guards," Artie said. "He wouldn't hire idiots who fall asleep on the job."

"My thoughts as well. Team One, proceed with caution."

With the go ahead, House and Sokolov moved down the dark alley, continuing their act of two lost tourists.

"You think this is the right way," House said.

"Good question. I lost the map," Sokolov responded.

"Team One, you're about twenty feet away. Let us know when you have a visual."

Team One continued their slow and playful approach. I knew they both had their hands near or on their weapons in the event things took a turn for the worse.

"Command, we have a visual," House whispered into the mic.

"Hello," she called out. "Can you help us? We're lost."

We heard no response, nor did we see any movement from the thermal imaging representing the two bodies. "Be careful, guys."

Team One was practically on top of the guards, and still we saw no response, but by that time, Kang and I had a pretty good idea why.

"Command, are you seeing what we're seeing? Can you confirm?"

"We are. And yes, it looks like both men have been decapitated."

"What?" Artie erupted. His voice reverberated in my earpiece. "They're dead?"

"Team Two, the entry guards have already been taken out. We need you to move in now with caution."

Kang switched the monitor to show a split screen of both video feeds. We watched Team Two make their way over to the target building and toward the stairwell. One of Artie's men produced a bolt cutter and snipped a lock on the door, and in they went.

"Command," House said, "the front door has been breached and it sounds uncharacteristically quiet inside.

We're moving inside the building."

We saw the bodies just inside the doorway at the same time as Team One did.

"Abby, you seeing this?" House asked as they stepped around the bodies.

"I am. Are you thinking what I'm thinking?" I asked.

"I am."

Kang motioned to me to shut my mic down.

"Don't tell me this is San Francisco all over again."

"It doesn't look good." When my supervisor had moved in to take down Jing Woo, the head of San Francisco's Triad gang and godfather of the city's Chinatown, they made the grim discovery that they were too late. All, with the exception of Jing, had been decapitated.

"Command, we're at the bottom of the stairwell on the fifth floor. We're using the fiber-optic video camera to get a look into the hallway."

A few seconds passed before Artie came back on the line. "The hallway looks completely empty."

"Are you sure?"

"Positive. We're moving forward."

Artie and his men pushed through the door with ease, since it wasn't locked, and made their way down the hall. Kang and I were able to see the hallway at that point via night vision feed from Artie's camera. Two of his men moved forward to the stairwell and held their position while Artie and the rest of his men stacked up next to the door to

Somchai's office. Before he could say anything, I did.
    "Let me guess: The door's already open."

Chapter 61

Inside, Artie found Somchai Neelapaijit in the same position that Reilly had discovered Jing Woo: on his back and opened up from sternum to pubic bone. His innards lay on the floor next to him, only this time, a piece of paper had been laid across Somchai's face with a typed message on it: *You can't stop the game.*

Kang and I exited the van and rallied with House and Sokolov before letting Artie's men know we were starting the five-floor walk up to Somchai's office. The stairwell was dark, and I wasn't sure if the building had any power until we reached the fourth floor where we could finally see light shining down from the fifth floor.

The lights in the office were on when we got there. I sort of wished they hadn't been. The amount of blood outside and inside the door gave me a visual of the sticky substance I had felt gripping the soles of my shoes as we traveled up the stairs. We had passed two bodies in the stairwell and a few others near the landings. Eventually, we had counted eight bodies. Those keeping an eye on our surveillance decoy were lucky that night.

Artie immediately called in manpower to have the

building cordoned off and secured. Somchai still had men loyal to him who were on the loose, and the last thing we wanted was to be surprised by anyone unfriendly.

Artie was at a loss for words as he surveyed the office. "How did this happen?"

"Trained hit men. Artie, we should move to apprehend the individuals watching our surveillance team. They might be next on the list, and they need to be questioned."

He nodded. "You're right. Word will spread fast." He made a call.

I made it clear to Artie that I wanted first dibs at an interview if they were successful at detaining any of the gang members or the two girls, considering his methods had resulted in the disappearance of the last guy. His pushback came as a surprise.

"Abby, I will be handling the interrogations. You are welcome to observe from a live video feed in another location."

Why not write a book about it, and I'll read it later when it's published? That's how I viewed his proposal. It was a little unfair, since we were supposed to be working together. But it was another reminder that we were in Bangkok only because the Thais had given us permission to be there.

I knew the amount of leeway Artie had already granted me was more than I should have been allowed. And I needed all the help I could get. Interviewing the remaining members of Somchai's crew could provide that.

"All I'm asking is to let me have a little time with them." I had lowered my voice and relaxed my posture, not wanting to challenge his authority as I had earlier that night at the restaurant. "I realize I have no call on this matter, but I'm asking you to please consider my request."

In the end, we compromised, sort of. "Okay, I'll give you two of them, but I'm picking them. Also, you get one hour for both. Take it or leave it?"

I took it.

As I had expected, all of Chinatown had shut down. Artie's supervisors and even their superiors showed up. I got the impression, even with all their posturing, that they were all unsure whether Somchai's death was a positive or a negative, but they needed to be there to support whatever the outcome. Politics.

Before the circus could balloon any bigger, I pulled Artie to the side and suggested that it would be best for the American entourage to take a back seat. He agreed and said he would try to steer any focus away from us. Under no circumstances did I want anyone within the Thai government to have the perception that we had spearheaded that operation.

In the end, the story that we fed everyone was that we had helped gather information, had provided tactical advice, and had supplied minimal surveillance support all at Artie's direction. He was in the limelight and in line for all the credit. I was happy to hand it over. My focus was still on the mastermind behind the game.

Chapter 62

As soon as we were released from the Somchai crime scene, House, Sokolov, Kang, and I reconvened in my room at the Landmark to discuss our next steps. We were tired, but time was working against us, as usual. Kang had room service bring up plenty of hot coffee and snacks. I dialed Reilly on the hotel phone and put him on speakerphone.

I spent the first fifteen minutes recapping what had happened. Reilly remained quiet the entire time, save for a few vocal acknowledgments every now and then. "Does our liaison at the embassy know what happened?" he asked when I finished.

"If you're asking if we had a conversation with him about this, then the answer is no," I said. "But I imagine it's only a matter of time before he gets wind of it. I thought I would check with you first to see how you wanted to play this."

"I appreciate your sensitivity on this matter. Let me deal with the embassy. It'll be better this way. As for what happened, are you sure we're not being looked at as troublemakers?"

"We're pretty sure; our presence is being looked upon

as minimal. The detective involved was all too eager to take credit for the operation."

"Fine. Let's talk next steps. What are your thoughts, Abby?"

I looked around the room at my partners before speaking. "It's clear to me that whoever is behind this game has no qualms about shutting it down in a particular city should it become a liability. They did it in San Francisco, and they did it again in Bangkok."

"So this doesn't mean the game is over, right?" Reilly asked.

"I doubt it. I think it means the city that was shut down is no longer in play. Whether it's indefinitely out of the game or not, who knows? But we have to assume it disrupts the dynamics of the game for the time being."

Kang cleared his throat. "Special Agent Reilly, this is Detective Kyle Kang speaking. The others are aware of this, but I don't believe you are. There are close to ninety established Chinatowns around the world. Only a handful of Chinatowns are being utilized for the game right now. Assuming the two are connected, the game could go live in any one of these cities."

"He's right," I added.

"The game is like a cockroach; you kill one, and five more appear." Reilly let out a loud breath.

"I wouldn't say it's exactly like that, but close. I'm thinking it's not that immediate. What we can do is advise law enforcement in the cities that are active in the game to target their Chinatown. Take out the management, and the game can't function."

"Either that or they get gutted like these last two guys," Reilly said.

"For some reason, I don't think the person responsible for this has hit men around the world on retainer with the ability to pull off what we witnessed here tonight," I said.

"We think one person or a group of them are sent to deal with a problem city," Kang chimed in. "They can't be everywhere at once. Shutting down the game in an active city will put us closer to shutting it down for good."

"So if Chinatowns are serving as the backbone or the network for this game, it's probably safe to assume that the Triads are behind it or somehow involved," Reilly suggested.

"I think you're right there," I said as I looked at Kang. He also had experience dealing with that organization. He nodded; he was on board with my assessment. "Kang agrees. I spent a great part of my career in Hong Kong locking up these hoodlums. They're extremely organized, have strongholds in all the major cities, and are financially healthy. They certainly have the means, but what I don't get is why. They're in the business of making money, like any other criminal organization. Why bother with this game?"

"She's right," Kang said. "Trafficking, prostitution, extortion, drugs, counterfeiting anything and everything…

that's their business. The game seems out of context for them."

Everyone around the phone nodded in agreement. If we were tying the game to Chinatown, it made perfect sense for the Triads to be involved. And yet it didn't. They cared about money. Was the game a moneymaker for them? Was there an exorbitant entry fee to play? If so, why would a serial killer pay money for the privilege to kill? Were they protected? Was it a safer route?

"We're all nodding over here," I reported to Reilly.

Reilly was quiet, but we could hear him tapping a pencil against his desk. The silence was more painful than it was deafening. And I mean that in an irritating way. "Do you have any concrete leads left in Bangkok?" he finally asked.

"If you're asking if we have someone to chase, no. But we do have some people we can interview. They could provide valuable information."

"Okay. Here's what we'll do. Agent House, Detective Sokolov, your purpose in Bangkok has been fulfilled. I want you two on a flight back to the States as soon as possible. Abby, how soon can you conduct your interviews?"

"I'm not sure. The Royal Thai Police are rounding up people of interest as we speak. As soon as—"

"So they're not currently in custody?"

"No, but—"

"And they might not be in custody?"

"Well, I'm sure—"

"Abby, I'm done making decisions based on 'what ifs.' You and Detective Kang can join your partners on the same flight home."

"But I'm sure they will be taken into custody at any moment, and talking to them could help us learn something of significance," I shot back. It took effort to keep my emotions in check and not let my voice rise. "These people worked with Somchai. They might have information that can lead us to the mastermind."

"Abby, this isn't a discussion. Say goodbye to the Big Mango. It's time to come home."

Before I could object, the line went dead.

Chapter 63

Silence blanketed the room. Had Reilly really just put an end to our investigation?

Kang was the first to voice his thoughts. "What now? We all go back to our jobs and forget about the game?"

All eyes settled on me. I knew House and Sokolov weren't invested in the case as Kang and I were. Their feelings would be neutral. They were in Bangkok because I had needed help, and it made sense for them to return home.

But ordering Kang and me to come back before we'd had a chance to follow up with Somchai's people, well, that was just Reilly asserting his authority and probably covering his ass should Somchai's death become political or should blame start to get thrown around. I got it. It's harder to point a finger at someone if they're not standing there in front of you. The sooner he had us back on US soil, the better.

"I'm sure he'll say we can keep working the case," I said, "but it'll be from our offices back in San Francisco."

"He probably thinks targeting overlords of the Chinatowns in the cities where the game is in play is akin to shutting down the game," House said with a shrug. "That bit of information sealed the deal here. Just saying."

I couldn't say that doing that wouldn't end the game. I mean, if the people who managed the game on a local level were taken out, how would the game continue? It would take time to replace those people. And sure, other cities could be activated, but that's all theory. The game could very well be limited to twenty cities.

Sensing my frustration, House, as usual, tried to help. "I'm sure we could stall for a day, maybe two at the most, but after that, it'll be hard to explain why we're not on a plane."

"I think the flights are full tomorrow," Sokolov added.

I should have said, "Thanks but no thanks," but that's not me, and they all knew it. Give me an inch and I'll take off and never look back. If they were willing to help buy me time for my interviews, I'd take it. I smiled at House and Sokolov before looking at Kang.

"I hurt my back last night," he said as he reached behind and rubbed himself. "I think I need to get it looked at before I subject myself to sitting in an airplane seat for fifteen hours."

I laughed because I was at a loss for words to describe my friends' willingness to rally around me. It was time to call Artie for an update. "Uh-huh, okay. Thanks, Artie. Let me know as soon as possible."

I put my cell back into my purse before addressing the group. "He hasn't heard anything yet, but he's sure his men were able to apprehend at least some of them. He said he would check and get back to me."

The "happy and hopeful" balloon in the room had deflated a tad with my news, but we had to remain positive. It made no sense for us to think Artie's men hadn't come through.

"Here's what we'll do," I said after a moment of thought. "Tracy, go ahead and make arrangements for us all to be on the same flight home in two days. Worst-case scenario, we don't have anyone to interview, and there's no need to be here."

"Got it." She pulled out her smartphone.

"In the meantime, I'll keep bugging Artie. Kyle, Pete, it's up to you what you want to do with your time from here on out."

Kang looked at Sokolov before addressing me. "We're fine waiting it out here with you. But I would suggest we all try to sleep for a few hours."

It was a little after two in the morning. Kang was right. I said goodnight to the three of them and watched them file out my door. I waited one minute before I picked up my cell phone and made a call.

"Artie, it's Abby. Where shall I meet you?"

Chapter 64

Artie had an unmarked car pick me up a half hour later.
I didn't recognize the driver, and he acknowledged me
without saying a word. As I opened the door to the front
passenger seat of the vehicle, he protested and pointed to
the back. I ignored him, sat down and closed the door.

I didn't get the impression he worked for the Royal
Thai Police. He wore an aged T-shirt, shorts, and no watch,
and his car smelled of garlic. This guy had been hired to
drive me, and that's it. Any further engagement would
garnish no useable information. I was content with staring
out the window.

On the ride to my undisclosed destination, I thought
about how I would keep this bit of information from my
partners, the people who had risked their lives that night for
my investigation. A tinge of guilt crept up my throat,
forcing me to swallow more than necessary. I had
essentially lied to them about my conversation with Artie,
but I'd had good reason.

The conversation that had taken place between the two
of us hadn't been anything like what it had sounded like on
my end. He'd had the individuals in custody and had

already transferred them to a location where he had already started his interrogation. I never did like that word. Connotations of torture filled my mind whenever I heard it. It's probably why I always referred to that process as an interview.

I knew firsthand that most questioning conducted by the authorities around the world, including those in Hong Kong, started out with a lot of physical contact. In the States, it was different—at least with the FBI. We had procedure, and it was followed very closely for a few good reasons. The rooms where people were detained and questioned were outfitted with video cameras and microphones to record everything that took place. The best reason, and probably the most effective, was that Americans loved to sue each other. Only a hint at stepping out of line, and threats of a lawsuit were paraded around.

But that wasn't the reason why I had withheld the truth of my conversation. Artie had, in fact, demanded that I not involve the others. It had been a last-minute addition to the conditions he had already set in place for my interview. I couldn't carry on a discussion without the others being privy, so I agreed. The fact that I'd heard a man screaming in pain in the background assured me that I had made the right decision.

Artie extracted information in a way that wasn't conducive to FBI or SFPD procedure. The way I saw it, I didn't need to involve my partners in a situation that could get them in trouble or, worse, get them fired. I was okay with putting my butt on the line but not someone else's. I'd endangered them enough with this investigation already. I felt I could explain my actions after the fact.

The driver drove me down a series of side streets. I didn't know where we were, but from the looks of it, we were deep inside a Thai neighborhood, far from the touristy Sukhumvit area that had surrounded me since my arrival.

There were no food vendors in sight, and I saw only the occasional person walking alongside the road. In addition, the lack of appropriate street lighting made every car, building, and stray dog we passed into a shadow. I'm sure I was the only non-Thai in the area.

He continued to weave the vehicle along the narrow road, making so many lefts and rights that it all appeared random to me, and I lost track of the direction we were heading. He had me completely turned around. Was that the goal?

Through the dirty passenger window, the condos and apartments I eyed gave way to small homes, which eventually gave way to shanties built out of rusted aluminum siding. Thirty minutes later, the vehicle stopped outside what seemed like a warehouse or a small factory— odd, even for a shanty neighborhood.

I stepped out of the vehicle and, for the first time since I had been in Thailand, I heard crickets singing, the occasional dog barking, and the rustle of tree leaves filled my ears. My driver led me down a pathway between the building and a wooden fence. Ten feet in, he stopped and motioned for me to pass.

The walkway was so narrow, even my tiny frame couldn't help but brush up against his equally small frame. He then opened a wooden door that swung in the opposite direction of where we stood, and I followed him into the dimly lit room. A musty scent with overtures of mechanical oil met my nostrils as we passed large pieces of machinery. It was too dark to make any further observations, and I prayed I didn't jab myself on something. That place was a lockjaw shot waiting to happen.

We continued through a series of doors and narrow halls until we reached a metal door. It was shortly after passing through that doorway that I heard screaming.

Chapter 65

The small room was hot and smelled as if one hundred men had relieved themselves inside it. A single low-wattage bulb lighted the windowless room, but I still spotted a slumped body in the corner—dead, from what I could tell. Of course, the man stripped of all his clothing and hanging from his arms was impossible to miss. His arms were tied together at the wrists above his head with rope, which was attached to a chained winch. There was no way he could stand on his own. His face resembled a squashed tomato, puffy and slick. Contusions covered most of his body.

"Cut that man down!" I shouted just as one of Artie's men coiled his arm back, ready to deliver another fistful of hurt. He stopped and turned toward me. His eyebrows were crunched, and his eyes were dark. He let out a dismissive breath before turning back to the task at hand. So did the other two men in the room, who seemed to be enjoying what had been taking place.

"Stop!"

I turned around and saw Artie sitting in a darkened corner behind me. I had been so shocked at what I had seen upon entering the room that I had completely missed him.

"Artie, this isn't right."

He stood up and walked toward me. He placed a hand on my shoulder. "Abby, this isn't America. Things are different here. This man is a criminal, a thug. He would rob, beat, and rape you without thinking about it."

I realized what Artie had said was the truth, but still, I wondered if he had tried talking first. "Look, I don't doubt your techniques produced the desired results. It's just that…"

"We have a different approach."

"Yes, I would say that."

Artie spoke in Thai to his men. One of them lowered the winch so the beaten man could sit in the chair moved into position by another man. They gave him some water.

"Let's step outside and talk," Artie said, motioning to the door.

I followed him into the hallway. "The guy lying in the corner, did you get any useful information from him?"

"No. He's there to help motivate the others when it's their turn to talk to us."

Yeah, that's working really well. I didn't want to get into a moral discussion, so I forced myself to keep the conversation tuned to the reason I was there. "Who am I interviewing? I want to get started right away."

"I had planned on giving you the girl who provided the answers to your riddles, but—"

"But what? She's fine. I'll take her." She was one of

my top picks for interviewing.

"She may look innocent, but she's not."

"I can handle myself."

"She attacked one of my men earlier. You're lucky she's still alive right now."

"What happened?"

"While they were transporting her here, she stuck a pencil into the throat of one of my men. They must have missed it during a pat-down." Artie looked down and shook his head before returning his attention to me.

"Is he okay?"

"He'll survive."

I couldn't believe what Artie had told me. That woman with the pixie frame and the large, doll-like eyes did that with a pencil? I shook my head. I didn't know what to say.

Artie led me farther down the hall to another door where one of his men stood guard. They had a short conversation before the guard unlocked the door, opening it cautiously. That room was also windowless but surprisingly brightly—lit by two fluorescent lightbulbs. The girl sat on the floor, huddled against the far wall. She was also stripped of most of her clothing, clad only in panties and a bra.

"Where are her clothes?" I asked, my anger rising.

Artie motioned with his head to a table in the corner where her clothes were. "Removing clothing can make them feel defenseless. Don't worry; my men don't do what you're thinking."

I grabbed her clothing and threw it over to her. "Get dressed."

Her bangs hung down over her eyes, but I could still see that she had swelling around one of them—a nice shiner. There was dried blood around her nostrils. One of Artie's men rolled a bottle of water toward her. She snatched it off the floor and drained it.

I turned to Artie. "Does she speak English?"

He shrugged.

"Hello," I said, keeping my tone soft. I took a step forward. "My name is Abby Kane. May I talk to you?"

I took another step closer. "Do you understand me?" I hoped she did. I wasn't keen on having Artie translate our conversation.

I looked at the guard. He had a scowl on his face— reason enough for this girl to not trust anyone. I also guessed he was the one who had socked her in her eye. "Let me try talking to her alone," I whispered to Artie.

"I don't think that's a good idea," he said, his voice low but stern. "She's dangerous."

"I understand that, but I think it might help if it were just the girl and me. Leave the door cracked. You'll still be able to hear everything that's discussed between us."

Artie bounced my proposal around in his head before agreeing to exit the room, leaving the door slightly ajar. He and his man stood outside, just as I had suggested.

When I turned back around, the girl had already closed

the gap between us and was seconds from colliding with
me.

Chapter 66

Instinctively, my right arm shot upwards. My hand, flat and rigid, cut into her throat. She fell to the floor, gripping her neck and choking for air. Artie and his guard rushed back into the room.

"What happened?"

"She got stupid, but I think I just smartened her up." I crouched near the withering girl, who was still fighting for every breath. "Misjudged me, didn't you?"

Surprisingly, she managed a few words, but they were in Thai. I looked at Artie with a raised brow, waiting for a translation.

"She asked if that's all you had in you."

I turned back to the girl. "This doesn't have to be hard. I just want to talk. Answer my questions, and I'm sure you'll be much happier about your situation because the alternative is not something you'll want."

When her coughing fit started to ease, I pulled her hands away from her throat. There was a bit of redness. "You'll be fine." I helped her into a sitting position. "Ready to talk?"

She nodded and coughed once more. I helped her to her

feet, walked her over to a chair, and sat her down. Artie handcuffed her wrists behind her back while I pulled up a small stool and sat in front of her a few feet away, in case she got stupid again.

"Do you understand me?" I asked. I didn't smile, but I softened my look. Even though I had karate-chopped her neck, I still needed the girl to engage with me.

She nodded.

"You know my name. Tell me yours?"

She swallowed and looked over my shoulder at Artie and his men.

"Sorry, I don't think I can convince them to leave this time."

"My name is Sei." Her voice wavered slightly.

"Well, Sei, I'm glad we're talking. I hope to get you out of here soon."

"Who's in charge? You or him?" She used her head to acknowledge between Artie and me.

"For now, let me ask the questions. Who told you to watch me?"

Her eyes shifted to the ground and then back to me. "My boss."

"Is your boss Somchai?"

She nodded.

"Why did he want you to watch me?" At the time, I thought it was better to leave Kang's name out of this conversation.

"I don't know, but he knew you were an FBI agent."

"So you provided him with information—what I did, where I went?"

"Yes."

"That's it?"

She nodded.

"I know you're involved with the game Chasing Chinatown. You gave me the answers to both riddles. What else do you know about the game?"

"My job was to provide the answers to the riddles."

"Was Somchai in charge of the game?"

The girl opened her mouth to speak but stopped. I repeated my question.

"Yes," she finally said. "He is a Deputy Mountain Master in charge of Bangkok."

I was familiar with the term she used. It was an elevated position in the Triad organization. That meant Somchai not only managed the game but also oversaw all Triad activity in Bangkok, probably in all of Thailand. Were the Triads really the ones behind this? Why? I still couldn't believe they would waste their time with a game unless it generated money.

"Did the Triads profit from the game?"

The girl shrugged.

"Did the players have to pay a fee to play?"

Again, she shrugged. That conversation was going nowhere fast. Either she had decided to keep quiet, or I was asking the wrong questions.

"How much control did Somchai have over the game?"

"It was his job to make sure the game ran smoothly in Bangkok."

"So there was someone else who controlled the game above him?"

She looked away and lowered her head.

"Sei, do you know who is in charge of the game?"

She shook her head slowly, still avoiding eye contact with me.

"Was Somchai responsible for approving the pictures that were uploaded in Bangkok?"

"No. He only passed them on to someone else for approval, but I don't know who that was. My job was to hand out answers. That's all."

"So you never saw or met the people Somchai reported to?"

"No."

We had made a little progress, I guess. She had confirmed what I had been thinking all along, that the overlords of each Chinatown managed the game on a local level but were not the creators or the ones in charge. They weren't even allowed to approve the pictures submitted. Was that left to the hands of the mastermind? Was the mastermind the head of the Triad organization—the Triads' top Dragon Head?

I looked down at my watch; time was running out. I

needed better information, something concrete. "I think you know more than what you're telling me. I need you to stop lying."

Her head perked up as her eyes widened. "I'm telling you the truth."

"I don't believe you, and that's a problem. It means I'll have to turn you over to these guys." I kept my eyes on her while I used my thumb to point over my shoulder.

"You have to believe me." Her breathing became elevated, and her eyes bounced around the room, searching for help. Both were signs that someone was telling the truth, but I knew she wasn't.

"Why do you insist on keeping up this charade of innocence?" I asked as I crossed my arms over my chest.

"I hand out answers. That's all."

"Stop lying."

"Somchai doesn't tell me anything."

"Yes, he does."

"This is all I know."

"No, it isn't."

"I'm just a girl working for money."

"Wrong!" My patience had run its course with her innocent act. "You were put in place to keep an eye on Somchai, weren't you?"

"I don't know what you're talking about."

"You reported to his boss. You knew everything he knew and more. Who killed Somchai? Who shut down him and the game in Bangkok? Who do you report to?" The level of my voice rose with each accusation that flew from my mouth.

She was lying. The responsibility of handing out the answers to the riddles was a bigger deal than she was making it seem. That position would require the person to have access to the game, to have knowledge of the riddles, to know what the tasks were, what the players looked like, and so on. Sei knew of all of this. Why was Sei given this access? Who was she? That's what I wanted to know.

"Tell me why you were placed in Bangkok. Was it to watch Somchai?"

She tried to rebuff my question. "Give me an answer!" I shouted.

I watched a light shade of crimson sour Sei's ivory-colored face as she tightened her jaw, forcing wet breaths to snake out between her teeth. "You can't win!" she hissed. "Your attempts to stop the game are futile!"

"I *will* put an end to this game," I countered with the same amount of fervor.

She threw her head back and cackled before settling back on me. With her eyes narrowed into dark slits, she lowered her voice. "Abby Kane, the hotshot FBI agent, you are no match for us. You are nothing but a gnat that we have enjoyed playing with, but now we've grown tired of you. Understand this: You cannot stop the game."

No sooner had those words left her mouth than her

right leg shot up, and her foot slammed into the side of my face, sending me flying off the wobbly stool and to land on the floor. I was dazed, but I was more surprised by her reach. I thought I had placed enough room between us.

I raised my arms, ready to fend off another attack, but none came. Instead, I watched her leap over me. Faster than anyone would have expected, she moved within striking distance of Artie and punted him in his crotch. In one fell swoop, she had immobilized the detective. I struggled to get to my feet, but the room turned on its axis, and I fell back down.

I watched Artie's man reach behind his back for his weapon, looking to put an end to the embarrassing debacle, but Sei shouted something in Thai that had him give pause. That little exchange gave her the upper hand. Her leg shot straight out and connected with his knee, hyperextending it and nearly dislocating it completely from the socket. With his leg bent in an unnatural direction and unable to bear his weight, he fell to one knee. A howl escaped his mouth, and his eyes squinted shut as Sei kicked his gun out of his hand.

Our innocent little girl had effectively taken out three law enforcement individuals, all while handcuffed. Sei wasn't a girl trying to make a living; she was a highly trained fighter.

Before she exited the room, she looked back at me with her hands still cuffed behind her back. She bent forward while sliding her hands down the back of her legs and down to her knees. She then plopped down on her butt and continued to slide her hands under her legs until she slipped them around the bottom of her feet. Her hands were now in front of her.

As she stood up, a smile stretched across her face. "Misjudged me, didn't you?"

Chapter 67

Artie was the first to recover and give chase. I wobbled after him but we were both too late; Sei had vanished. Somehow, she had made her way out of the building and disappeared into the surrounding dwellings—still handcuffed but definitely much more mobile than we were. Artie ordered the rest of his men to search the area. I watched as they fanned out and disappeared into the night.

"She couldn't have gotten far," Artie said, turning back toward me. "We'll find her."

"Really? We underestimated her once. Let's not embarrass ourselves further by doing it again."

Artie's nostrils flared as he dismissed my statement, but he knew I spoke the truth. That girl was long gone, probably already doubling back or circling around to cover her tracks. I suspected Artie's men would come up empty-handed.

We had all grossly misread her, and she had capitalized on that. Shame on us. The whole ordeal angered me; I should have known better. I had gained many advantages over my opponents because they had underestimated my abilities due to my short stature.

"Height is an advantage, Abby. Don't forget that," my father had always told me. When he'd said that, I had always thought it only applied to me and not to others. Now I knew I wrong. *Sorry, Dad.*

"Your questions toward the end—those are what set her off." Artie walked back to where I stood. "Why did you suspect that she was more than just a low-level employee?"

"The Triads don't usually use women in that manner. I believe she was placed there primarily to keep an eye on Kang and I, but she was also to watch over Somchai. It explains how someone got to him before we did. She was a mole."

"So what is she, some hired assassin?"

"That would be my first guess, but for some reason, my gut tells me she's loyal to one person in the Triads, or to the Triads as a group. I don't get the feeling she's a gun for hire. One thing's for sure: She'll report what happened here tonight to her boss, whoever that might be."

"Somchai must have done something to warrant his death."

"I'm guessing kidnapping me and telling me about the Creeper wasn't a smart thing, especially if it wasn't sanctioned. That's not how the Triads operate. They're sticklers for procedure. He would have needed to inform his superiors if there were a problem."

I let out a yawn before looking at my watch. It was nearing five in the morning; it would be daylight soon.

"I'm sorry about the way this turned out," Artie said. "I'm not sure you got anything out of it except a kick to the face."

"I'm happy it wasn't the same side of my face that the Creeper chose to beat," I said with a chuckle. I don't bruise easily, but I do swell. Signs of the beating I had taken from the Creeper had disappeared by the following day, and the tenderness had all but vanished. The side of my face that had been kicked felt warm but not swollen. "It's not that bad."

Artie nodded and looked around. It was just the two of us. It was quiet except for the shuffling of our feet on the asphalt. The driver who had brought me here appeared from the side of the building. He must have been inside the whole time.

"You should go back to your hotel and get some rest. There's nothing for you to do here. This is my mess to clean up."

I couldn't have agreed more. And I had no intention of helping Artie find his missing girl or explain the dead body inside the building. That was all him. I walked over to the front passenger side of the car. "I'm sorry, too," I said before getting inside.

Artie pocketed his hands in his pants and rocked on his

heels as he watched the black sedan drive away. He had underestimated the girl, but how could he have known? At least, that was how he had rationalized it in his head. He wasn't too broken up about it. It looked like he would be getting credit for taking down Somchai Neelapaijit earlier in the night, even though he'd had nothing to do with the leader's death. This little mishap, as he considered it, could easily be buried and forgotten about. Somchai will be the focus, not his underlings.

Artie turned around to walk back toward the building but instead found himself face to face with the girl his men were out hunting.

"You didn't think I would leave with these on, did you?" Sei held her hands up, the metal cuffs twinkled in the moonlight.

Before Artie could even hint at any attempt of restraining her, she had pivoted around him and jumped on his back. Her thin legs locked around his chest for balance as she slipped her hands over his head, hooking the handcuffs underneath his chin and into the crook of his neck.

Artie managed to grab her hands and pull in an effort to prevent her from choking him, but she was faster. She had already released her leg lock and maneuvered them both behind his back. She pulled, drilling her knees into his back for leverage. He tried to slip a finger underneath the chain of the handcuffs to create separation from his throat, but it was too tight.

Artie twisted and rocked his torso, trying anything to buck her off or at least disrupt the leverage she was creating, but she clung to him like a stubborn barnacle. She maneuvered her feet until both were placed flat against his back. He felt her begin to straighten out her body, pulling her handcuffs tighter against his neck and driving the hard metal of each cuff deeper into his soft flesh.

The force toppled them backward, and he landed on Sei, but she still managed to keep both of her feet firmly planted on his back as she rolled them over to the side. While his legs flailed, his fists battered her arms relentlessly, hoping to create even the tiniest break in her grip. Nothing he did appeared to have any effect on her. She was a machine, but Artie refused to give up. He fought and fought. With each blink, the night sky grew darker during a time when he knew the sun should have been rising until all there was left for him to see was the blackness of death.

Chapter 68

After grabbing a few hours of much-needed sleep, I joined the rest of my team for a late lunch. As far as I knew, no one had any idea that I had left the hotel to meet with Artie, but it was time to come clean. On the way down to the lobby, I tried to formulate how I would broach the subject. Everything that popped into my head sounded very silly. The best approach would be honesty.

When I entered the hotel restaurant, I saw the others sitting at a table. They had already made a pass at the buffet and were digging in. Kang saw me first.

"Abby, what happened to your face?" he said, wiping his mouth with a cloth napkin.

"I can explain." A nervous chuckle followed. I wasn't looking forward to what I had to say next. "Last night, I met up with Artie."

All at once, they stopped stuffing their faces and gave me their full attention. No one said anything, but their eyes told me they were looking for an explanation.

House spoke up first. "Abby, you should have told us you were meeting with him," she said, her tone direct. I didn't blame her for being worried.

"I know."

"We're a team. We look out for each other. Our strength is in our numbers, too, not just our brains," she continued.

"I'm sorry. I didn't want to involve any of you in Artie's shady tactics for extracting information. I knew you guys wouldn't have cared, but we're already stepping on eggshells here." I told them Artie had already started interrogating the gang members when he called because I could hear screaming in the background.

"Regardless, Abby, you should have told us. And if the deal was for you to fly solo, at least we would have known you were with Artie," Kang said as he stabbed a piece of bacon with his fork and shoved the entire thing into his mouth.

"You're right."

"Did you learn anything useful from your interview?" he asked as he chewed noisily.

"I got information, but I don't know if it's useful yet."

They listened intensely as I recapped the early-morning events.

Kang responded first. "The shop girl, the innocent-looking one that gave us our answers, is an assassin?"

"It's a pretty good assessment considering the abilities she displayed."

Kang ran his hand through his hair as he tried to make sense of what I said. The others looked just as dumbfounded.

"I also wasn't expecting to hear that." House tilted her head to the side before spooning fresh-cut pineapple into her mouth. "The dead body, the beatings—that wasn't a surprise."

"This girl adds a new dimension to the investigation," I said. "Do we focus on her? Was she really a plant or just hired help? Does she know the mastermind?"

"What's the first thing that popped into your head?" Kang asked.

"That she was inserted into Somchai's crew to keep an eye on him. And if I'm right, that means somebody expected a problem and wanted a solution in place."

"Maybe we're more of a threat to the game than we think," Kang said between bites.

"Then why let us play? It doesn't make sense."

"I agree," House said. "And what makes even less sense is that the end result was them having to eliminate their own people and shut down the game play in Bangkok. How is that helpful?"

"Maybe they weren't expecting that." Kang pointed his fork at me.

"You might be right there. Sei did indicate that, in the beginning, entertainment was the driving factor in letting us play."

"Boy, these people are really dumb. Because they let us play the game, they lost two cities and three teams."

Sokolov swallowed and then cleared his throat. "Are we positive the game is finished here?"

I shrugged. "It's more of an assumption. We think Somchai managed the game. With him dead and his crew in shambles, who's left to run the game? I don't think it's a big deal for them to shut down a city. Really, they can still play the game with the eighteen other cities."

"Or open up a new city," Kang added. "Plenty of untapped Chinatowns."

"You know, Abby, you still have the other plan that Reilly's implementing—taking out the management in the remaining Chinatowns. It's a lot easier to target the person in charge than to find the killers."

"I don't disagree. It's the best plan we have. And honestly, if the game becomes a pain, these players will abandon it. That by itself could effectively shut the entire game down. It won't, however, deliver us the mastermind."

I looked around the table and knew what they were all thinking: Reilly was already putting the best plan into motion, and the discovery of this girl didn't trump it. Even if I did think she had ties to the mastermind, I couldn't prove it, and to make matters worse, I had no idea where she was. Sei had become a ghost, as Reilly would have put it.

"I need to eat," I said, breaking the silence. I got up and headed to the buffet. It wasn't often I walked away from a lead, but I had walked away from that one. There just wasn't enough there.

I headed straight for the buffet table with the fruit and zeroed in on the platter loaded with papaya. I scooped up nearly half of the dark orange pulp onto my plate before making the rounds to see what else could tempt a second trip. Before I could return to the table, my cell rang. I recognized the number. It was Special Agent Jacob Brewer, my contact at the embassy. *Shoot! I thought Reilly had talked to him.*

"Agent Brewer, how can I help you?"

"It's imperative that you and your team leave the country immediately."

"We have flights booked tomorrow night, and—"

"Not good enough, there's a chartered flight leaving tonight. I'll get you guys on it."

"What's going on, Agent?"

"Your detective friend, Songwut Soppipat—"

"You mean Artie?"

"It's unofficial, but my sources tell me he was found dead this morning."

"What? How can that be? I—"

"Don't say anything, Agent Kane. I don't want to know. I'm not saying you were involved or had previous knowledge of this, but in the event that the Thai authorities think otherwise, it's best we field their questions on our turf."

"But we didn't do—"

"Not another word, Agent. Inform your team and wait for my instructions. Is that understood?"

"Yes."

Chapter 69

Returning home and seeing my family had been a mix of emotions. One: I was scared to death to face Lucy and Ryan. I worried that, in a single phone call, I had undone all the trust I had built with them, and we would return to being the strangers that we had been when we first met. Two: I loved them so much it hurt. All I wanted then was to hug them and never let go.

Happily, I had been worried over nothing.

Both children welcomed me back with large smiles. Lucy practically leaped into my arms the minute I opened the front door, almost toppling me. Ryan, who usually stood off to the side waiting until Lucy had received her hugs and kisses, was right behind her and joined in with a bear hug of his own. To my surprise, even Po Po gave me a welcome-back hug. She had also prepared a special five-course dinner of all my favorite dishes. I felt so loved at that moment. I had been so focused on my love for them and whether I had given enough, I didn't realize they had an equal amount to return to me.

We talked a little about that phone call over dinner but didn't dwell on it. Clearly, what mattered to my family was that I was home. The past was the past, and we needed to relish the moment and look forward to the future. I had forgotten how resilient kids were.

I spent the rest of the night listening to stories about what I had missed while I was away. They both talked about school and their friends. Lucy had reenrolled in dance classes and had prepared a special performance for me. Ryan showed off his latest judo moves and the new kung fu outfit for the lessons he would soon start.

That night was a smattering of their lives, whatever popped into their minds. It didn't matter to me. I wanted to hear every detail. Nothing was mundane. It was all worthy as far as I was concerned.

I returned to the office two days later to find that the Thai authorities had come knocking on our door for answers. When the embassy had notified them that we had already jetted out of the country on a diplomatic charter plane, they weren't too happy. I didn't blame them; one of their best detectives had been murdered.

In the following days, I was happy to answer questions and fill in the blanks. I had done my best to be completely forthcoming with the events of that night, everything from the interrogations to the girl escaping. I considered Artie a friend, and it still shocked me that he had been killed. I didn't want to impede their investigation; I wanted to help them. I wanted them to bring his killer to justice.

According to the Royal Thai police, when Artie's men

returned from their search, they had found him unconscious and not breathing. They administered first aid but had failed to revive him. I told them it had to be the girl, Sei. Artie had been alone when I left. She could have easily doubled back and attacked him.

They agreed, and their findings also pointed to the girl. Handcuffs had been found next to Artie's body, the ones we'd used to restrain her. The medical examiner's report only reinforced it.

Tip had personally handled the autopsy, and she was nice enough to forward a copy of it directly to me. Her official report stated that Artie had died from ligature strangulation. Pictures of Artie's neck showed bruising that was in line with the markings of a cuff and part of a chain. I sent her a short email with my condolences and told her that, if she needed any information from me regarding the case, she needn't hesitate to reach out.

I also went ahead and worked up a profile on the girl in hopes that it might help the Thai police. I could paint an idea of how she thought and what her motivations might be. They had no record of Sei in their files; this was their first encounter with her, so any information was helpful.

I had my doubts that they would find her, not for lack of ability but more because of who they were dealing with. A seasoned assassin would know how to disappear and remain invisible for as long as needed. I'd be surprised if Sei were still in Thailand.

With that all said, I still wasn't ready to just sit back and see how the case shook out, even when my involvement in the investigation had diminished due to the fact that we didn't have any players to catch in the US. I had time on my hands, and I did exactly what Reilly had told me: "Abby, if you want to catch the mastermind, you need to catch him with your brain, not with force. That's your strength. Use your head."

I took what he had said seriously and spent my time at the office expanding my profile on Sei. I also did my best to dig up any information I could on her. I even reached out to an old friend back in Hong Kong, Leslie Choi, my protégé who had taken over my old position as Inspector in charge of the Organized Crime and Triad Bureau.

"Abby!"

A squeal erupted from my phone loud enough that I had to pull it away from my ear, but I still held my grin. "Hi, Leslie."

"I thought you had run off to live in the mountains as a hermit. You never answer my emails."

"I know, I know. Bad habit I have, but I'm calling and that's a whole lot better."

"It is, but a visit would be better. Oh, wait. Tell me you're calling to let me know you're coming to Hong Kong."

I chuckled. "I wish I were coming to see you. It's long overdue."

"I second that. So what do you need?"

"What makes you think I need something?"

"Abby? Come on…"

"All right, I just didn't want it to be all business."

"I've already heard your sweet voice. I'm good for another couple years."

We both laughed, and I gave Leslie a quick overview of the case and the girl, Sei.

"Dammit. You always end up with the interesting cases!"

"It's all packaging my friend, all packaging. So have you heard of this girl?"

"Name doesn't ring a bell personally, but that doesn't mean we don't have something on her. I'll poke around and see what I can come up with."

"Thanks, Leslie. I appreciate it."

We talked for a bit longer. I told her about life in San Francisco, and how the kids and Po Po were doing, and what being an agent for the FBI was really like. She couldn't believe that I primarily investigated white-collar crimes, financial stuff. "Believe it. This case is an anomaly. Most of my time is spent chasing greedy bankers."

"Well, I guess it's best for the new Abby Kane and family," she laughed. "No, seriously, I'm happy for you. Family is important."

"Speaking of family, do you have a man? You kind of need one of those to get one started."

"I'm working on it."

Oh, I almost forgot: I worked the case with Kyle Kang."

"The detective?"

"Yup."

"If I remember correctly, he was a pretty smart guy— good-looking, too. Listen, I hate to cut our call short, but duty calls."

"I understand. Take care my friend."

"You, too."

After I hung up with Choi, I thought about how our friendship had changed after I had moved to the States. Actually, the correct word would be "suffered," and it saddened me. But I also knew I was happier in life. Nothing could trump being a parent. And yet, somehow, every now and then, my job did just that.

I had known the deal when I signed on to work for Reilly. I would spend most of time investigating white-collar crime and the occasional serial killer/gang-related investigation would be thrown my way. It would disrupt the Kane household for a bit, but I could live with that. Sort of.

Chapter 70

The front doors to the Hop Sing Tong in San Francisco's Chinatown had been chained shortly after the FBI had finished their investigation. Control of the building had reverted to the Chinese organization that owned it, but from that day forward, not a single person had been seen entering or exiting the building, and its windows remained dark at night.

The residents, particularly those who owned shops and restaurants along Waverly Street, wondered if perhaps the building had been sold. If so, who were the new owners, and why had nobody heard anything about it? A sale of such a property would have to be approved by the other benevolent associations or tongs that helped govern the neighborhood of course. An exchange of hands was highly unlikely, but no one could be sure.

"Abandoned" was the word that populated the daily gossip regarding the building. It was believable, too, except a shopkeeper swore he had seen a small light flicker on in one of the windows, if only for a brief moment. It didn't matter whether the others believed that to be true, because shortly after he made his claim, the chains that secured the tong's doors were removed, the sidewalk out front was swept clean, and late at night, a light could be seen emanating from a window on the top floor.

Yet even with these obvious signs of life, there was still no sighting of who had recently come to occupy the tong.

But someone had.

Chapter 71

With three weeks having passed since my return from Thailand, I had regained a sense of normalcy in my life. The workload at the office had returned to manageable levels and hours, allowing me to effectively parent again. I wasted no time in embracing the routine of family life I had so missed while buried in the Chasing Chinatown investigation.

A big part of that routine consisted of Ryan joining me on my trips to the gym when he didn't have a class at the dojo. Conditioning was our focus, and we would always spar a little, but what he had really taken a liking to was something my father always wished I had taken a larger interest in: grappling.

A while ago, I had shown Ryan a couple of moves I had learned from my father and the FBI academy. I hadn't realized that he had spent a great deal of time practicing the moves until I got a call from the school a few days ago. Ryan had got in a fight.

My first thought while I drove there to pick him up was, *What on Earth are you doing fighting in school?* I worried that maybe my being away was the culprit. I worried that my not being around led to him falling into the wrong group of friends. I worried that this might be the beginning of a troubled childhood.

I was wrong. There was a bully, and Ryan had taught him a lesson.

Turns out, this kid had been picking on my son for the last two months, but Ryan had done what I had always told him to do: He took the high road. Long story short, the kid kept on bullying Ryan, and it got out of control. His side of the story was that he had no choice but to defend himself.

"It was after school. He and his friends had circled around me," Ryan said. "I swear, Abby, I tried to talk my way out of it. But he charged me. I had to protect myself."

And that's exactly what Ryan had done. I had taught him a simple submission move: the Guillotine Choke Hold. It's very easy to execute when your opponent charges with his head down. Basically, it's a reverse headlock.

"He came at me head down and I wrapped my arm under his neck…"

I'll be honest, hearing Ryan describe how he successfully executed a submission move—one that I had taught him—on a kid who was *taller* and *heavier* than him, well, let's just say it had me beaming with mommy pride and delivering high fives like there was no tomorrow. This was all on the inside of course. On the outside, I was Abby the Parent. My left eyebrow had arched into a fine point while my mouth muttered something about being grounded for a week.

Ryan had slipped his arm under the charging kid's chin and yanked up against his throat. He then grabbed that wrist with his free arm and pulled upward, while falling back.

"You should have seen it, Abby. Once we were on the ground, I wrapped both legs around his torso and pushed his hips down, creating the force I needed, but I was careful not to knock him out. I just held him until some other kids could call a teacher."

That move earned Ryan a two-day suspension, but had he actually choked the kid out, I'd probably be looking for a new school for him to attend, and I would have some very angry parents to deal with.

Dealing with Ryan's first schoolyard fight reminded me of mine. My tormentor was Mei Lin. She was a year older, sixteen, had big floppy breasts that the boys loved, and never liked me from day one. As usual with kids, these things almost always come to a head.

I remembered that the first words out of my father's mouth when he arrived at my school weren't "Are you okay?" but "Did you win?" I had known there was only one answer he wanted to hear. I hated to admit it, but it was the same answer I wanted to hear from Ryan.

As for the case, I spent most of my time advising law enforcement officials in other countries. Because I still had access to Team Carlson's account—don't ask me why, I could track the players via the live updates in the game. Any information I could provide that helped them track their killer was welcomed.

Aside from that, I also advised them to subpoena the tongs and search any computers, smartphones, and tablets they found for the Chasing Chinatown game. They could try to gain access to the game themselves, discover the Attractions for their city, and tie them into any recent murders. That could help prove a connection between the tong and a murder victim. Of course, in the end, I told them there was no one single way to shut the game down and not to discount going after the team in their city.

The Merseyside Police in Liverpool proved just that. Between my help and that of the United Kingdom's Security Service—MI5—they were actually able to catch Team Loathe. They then gained access to their account via their laptop and did exactly what Kang and I had done— played the game. Within a week, they had arrested the Deputy Mountain Master who ran Liverpool's Chinatown and effectively shut down the game in their city.

One by one, the Triad organizations in the cities connected to the game were dismantled, and any live updates of a team's progress in that city stopped immediately. That alone told us we were disrupting the game play. We may not have been making the strides needed to catch the mastermind, but we were at least taking away a reason for a bunch of sickos to run around the world killing people.

◇◇◇

It was a late Tuesday morning, and I was busy monitoring the game while I munched on a lox bagel and sipped tea at my desk. The office was busy with plenty of foot traffic around me, but I had my ear buds in, and I quietly rocked out while I worked. A phone call on my cell stopped the party though.

"Abby, it's Kyle. What's the latest?"

"I got word that the Netherlands National Police Service raided the Chinatown in Amsterdam. Since then, I've been paying special attention to any activity in that city. None so far."

"That's great news. We're down to ten cities now?"

"Yeah…"

"Aw, come on. You've got to be happy about this."

"I am. It's bittersweet."

"I hear you. The icing on the cake would be nabbing the a-hole who created this game."

"Bingo!"

"I don't mean to abruptly change the subject, but I am going to. You'll never guess what showed up at the precinct."

"Dim sum?"

"Well, yeah, I did order some. But that's not what I wanted you to guess."

"Huh?"

"Forget about what I just said. Listen, I just received an invitation to attend the grand reopening of the Hip Song Tong."

"That's the tong Reilly busted a couple months ago."

"Apparently they've turned over a new leaf. They're having a big celebration and inviting people to come to an open house. They'll have food and entertainment and other stuff. Should be interesting."

"You want me to tag along?"

"Yeah, and bring the family, too. They'll have games and rides. Plus, your Po Po can get in a day's worth of gossip."

"I am curious about who's now in charge of that place. Count me in."

After I hung up with Kang, I gave Reilly the heads up about the tong and asked if he wanted to attend the street fair.

He declined but agreed that it was a good idea for me to go. "Keep your eyes open, Abby. That place has been dormant since our raid. I find it odd that they're suddenly having a family-friendly, fun-filled festival."

I returned to my desk and again checked for any activity in Amsterdam. There was none. I felt pretty good about notifying the KLPD that they had successfully shut the game down, until a message window appeared within the game and stopped me in my tracks. I'd had no idea the game had messaging capabilities until that day. But what I found even more surprising was the message itself.

Anonymous: Hello, Agent Kane.

What the hell? I stared at the screen for a few moments wondering if this was my doing, but I quickly tossed the thought. *Do I respond? Ignore? Who could this be?* I picked up my laptop and headed straight for Reilly's office. He had his nose buried in his smartphone when I closed the door behind me.

"Is something wrong?" He scrunched his eyes as he removed his glasses.

I balanced my laptop on a stack of manila folders piled on his desk. "The game just messaged me."

"What?" Reilly leaned in for a closer look. "When did this happen?"

"About thirty seconds ago."

Reilly pointed at the screen. "Respond."

Team Carlson: This is Agent Kane. Who am I speaking to?

Anonymous: You were warned in Bangkok.
Team Carlson: Warned about what?
Anonymous: You cannot stop the game. No one can.

I looked at Reilly. "What do you think?"

"We have the attention of the mastermind. Clearly, our strategy of shutting down the game by taking out the Chinatowns is working."

"This is nothing but a smokescreen."

Reilly nodded his agreement.

Team Carlson: I hate to destroy your fantasy, but we are shutting the game down.

A minute passed without a response. "Is that it?"

Reilly shrugged. "Keep engaging."

Team Carlson: You're quiet because you know we speak the truth.

Anonymous: I'm quiet because I'm laughing. Agent Kane, I'll grant your wish.

Team Carlson: And what's that?

Anonymous: You are officially a player in the game.

Team Carlson: I didn't need your approval in the past. Why do I need it now?

Anonymous: Because the rules have changed. One city. One Attraction.

Team Carlson: That makes our job easier. Good luck.

Anonymous: No, Agent. It is you who will need the well-wishing.

Reilly and I waited, but no other communication came

through, even after more prompting.

"One city. One Attraction. Did they really just consolidate the game to one city?" Reilly crossed a leg over the other as he leaned back in his chair.

I minimized the message window so we could see the map of the world. A city in play was marked by a red dot, and there was only one left on the map: San Francisco.

"Wait. Our city is back in the game?" I clicked on the marker, and the screen zoomed in to our location. A title appeared: *Welcome to San Francisco.*

Instead of seeing the original five completed Attractions, there was only one. I clicked on the heading, and a graphic of a paper scroll appeared. It unraveled, revealing a message along with a picture of me.

> *No riddle. Just one task:*
> *Kill FBI Agent Abby Kane.*
> *Win $10,000,000!*
> *Good luck, teams.*

This concludes *Lumpini Park*, book two in the Chasing Chinatown trilogy. Stay tuned for the final installment, *Coit Tower*. Abby Kane becomes the sole objective of the game and the target for its players. Can she take down the mastermind before the players take *her* down?

A Note From Ty Hutchinson

Thank you for reading LUMPINI PARK. If you're a fan of Abby Kane, spread the word to friends, family, book clubs, and reader groups online. You can also help get the word out by leaving a review on Amazon. If you do leave one, send me an email with the link. Or if you just want to tell me something, email me anyway. I love hearing from readers. I can be reached at thutchinson@me.com.

Better yet, sign up for my Super Secret Newsletter and receive "First Look" content. Be in the know about my future releases and what I'm up to. There will even be opportunities to win free books and whatever else I can think of. Oh, and I promise not to spam you with unnecessary crap or share your email address. Sign up now at http://eepurl.com/zKJHz.

There's a lot of procedure in the FBI, and I don't always stay true to it. If I leave something out or change the way things are done, it's because I don't think it helps the story. A dear friend of the family is a retired FBI agent, and that person does a pretty good job of keeping me in check, both verbally and with eye rolls. But in the end, I write what makes the story better, and that's the way it is. After all, this is fiction.

I tend to hang out in these places. Stop by.
Blog: http://tyhutchinson.wordpress.com/
Facebook:
http://www.facebook.com/tyhutchinson.author

The Novels of Ty Hutchinson

Abby Kane FBI Thrillers
Corktown
Tenderloin
Russian Hill (CC Trilogy #1)
Lumpini Park (CC Trilogy #2)
Coit Tower (CC Trilogy #3)
Kowloon Bay
Suitcase Girl (SG Trilogy #1)
The Curator (SG Trilogy #2)

Sei Assassin Thrillers
Contract: Snatch
Contract: Sicko
Contract: Primo
Contract: Wolf Den
Contract: Endgame

Darby Stansfield Thrillers
Chop Suey
Stroganov
Loco Moco

Other Thrilling Reads

Made in the USA
Monee, IL
01 December 2020